A CRIME IN TIME

"If only there was a way we could prove you didn't steal the tea set," Catherine said with a sigh.

"Yeah, but how?" Frank asked.

"I don't know exactly." Catherine began to pace. Suddenly she stopped, her eyes wide. "How about all those crime stories I read in the *Police Gazette* and the way the cops track down the gangsters? We can do the same thing!"

"Forget it," Frank said. "A mug like me is always catching the heat. I shoulda known I'd be kicked out sooner or later."

Suddenly Catherine saw that Frank's diary was glowing. "Frank, look!" she shouted, pointing to the diary. It glowed brighter and brighter. "What is it?"

Frank stared at the diary in shock. "Beats me," he finally whispered.

"Let's get out of here!" Catherine cried. She ran for the stairs.

JOIN THE TEAM!

Do you watch GHOSTWRITER on PBS? Then you know that when you read and write to solve a mystery or unravel a puzzle, you're using the same smarts and skills the Ghostwriter Team uses.

We hope you'll join the team and read along to help solve the mysterious and puzzling goings-on in all of the GHOSTWRITER books!

JUST IN TIME

A Novelization by
Fracaswell Hyman
Based on his own teleplay

A Children's Television Workshop Book

Bantam Books
New York Toronto London Sydney Auckland

JUST IN TIME
A Bantam Book/January 1996

Ghostwriter, **Ghost**writer and ◉ are
trademarks of Children's Television Workshop.
All rights reserved. Used under authorization.
Cover design by Marietta Anastassatos.
Cover photo of clock: THE STOCK MARKET/
Lightscapes.

ISBN 0-553-48271-8

Published simultaneously in the United States and Canada

Bantam Books are published by Bantam Books, a division of Bantam Doubleday
Dell Publishing Group, Inc. Its trademark, consisting of the words "Bantam
Books" and the portrayal of a rooster, is Registered in U.S. Patent and Trademark
Office and in other countries. Marca Registrada. Bantam Books, 1540 Broadway,
New York, New York 10036.

PRINTED IN THE UNITED STATES OF AMERICA

OPM   0   9   8   7   6   5   4   3   2   1

Ghostwriter doesn't know where he came from. He doesn't remember who he was when he was alive. He can communicate only using written words. His friends Jamal, Lenni, Gaby, Alex, and Tina are the only people who can see his glowing words. He has helped them solve lots of mysteries. Now he's being taken away from them. Whisked through a tunnel of swirling newspaper print. Pulled faster and faster by the words *HELP* . . . *SCARED* . . . *TROUBLE* . . .

In a basement, twelve-year-old Frank Flynn writes in his diary. Frank is very upset and doesn't notice Ghostwriter's swirling glow as it lands and sweeps across the words he's been writing.

Help! I'm scared*!*
I'm in trouble!
I didn't do it!

Chapter 1

Jamal Jenkins was stretched out on his bed reading a mystery when his friend Lenni Frazier burst into the room waving a piece of paper. "Guess who I got a letter from?"

"Rob?" Jamal asked eagerly, sitting up.

Lenni nodded. "Yeah. He says he likes Australia. But he still wishes he could have spent summer vacation here in Brooklyn with the team."

"We're not much of a team without Ghostwriter." Jamal sighed sadly and closed his book.

"I know," Lenni said. "Rob asked about Ghostwriter in his letter. He wants to know if he's back yet. He's worried about him."

"Me too," Jamal said. "Ghostwriter's been

gone for two whole weeks. What if he's in trouble or can't find his way back?"

Lenni sat on the edge of Jamal's bed. "That's why I came over. We're still a team and we have a mystery to solve."

"What mystery?"

"We need to find out where Ghostwriter is and get him to come back. We *need* him. And he might need us, too."

"You're right," Jamal said, walking over to his desk. "I'm gonna call a rally and get the team on the case!" He picked up a pen and wrote on a memo pad *"RALLY J."*

Lenni laughed. "Jamal, *what* are you doing?"

"Calling a rally." Jamal felt foolish when he realized what he'd done. "Oh . . . I guess we can't do that without Ghostwriter."

"Right," Lenni said. "We're going to have to get the team together the old-fashioned way—by telephone."

In the living room of the Canellan house, twelve-year-old Catherine and her younger sister, Lucy, fidgeted as they listened to their housekeeper, Mrs. O'Boyle, complain. "That tea set was your mother's most cherished possession. I polished it every week, just the way she did before she died."

"We know, Mrs. O'Boyle," Catherine said,

rolling her eyes. She was growing tired of the housekeeper's constant griping.

Mrs. O'Boyle continued chattering away angrily. She didn't see Frank and the girls' father, Dr. Canellan, walking into the living room. "She wanted you girls to be able to pass it on to your children," Mrs. O'Boyle continued. "That'll never happen now, thanks to that no-good thief Frank."

"Hey, I'm no thief!" Frank said, his face turning red.

Mrs. O'Boyle spun around and glared at him. She turned toward Dr. Canellan. "I'm sure the tea set was here this morning before Frank left the house." She sniffed.

"Yes, but that doesn't prove Frank took it," said Dr. Canellan.

"What about the glove?" ten-year-old Lucy asked with a smirk.

"That's right," Mrs. O'Boyle said. She smiled at Lucy and patted her arm. "One of Frank's work gloves was lying on the floor right next to the breakfront. Lucy found it."

"It must've fell out of my pocket," Frank insisted.

"Or someone could have put it there," Catherine said as she stared accusingly at her red-haired little sister. "Someone could be trying to make it look as if Frank is guilty. But that still doesn't prove anything."

Lucy glared at Catherine and stomped out of the room. Everyone sat silently for a minute.

"Dr. Canellan," Mrs. O'Boyle finally said, "I know you have a soft spot in your heart for orphans and their troubles, but Frank was a thief the first time we laid eyes on him. He was halfway out the upstairs window with a bag full of loot, including the silver tea set. He should be thrown back out into the streets where he came from."

"Horsefeathers!" blurted Catherine. "This just doesn't make any sense. Frank does his chores. He tries hard in school. He even helps fix things." Catherine walked over to Frank. "You like living here, don't you, Frank?"

Frank glanced around the large, comfortable living room. "Sure, this is the swellest place I've ever lived."

"And what did Father say would happen to you if you were ever, ever caught stealing again?"

"He said he would kick me out," Frank muttered.

"See!" Catherine said, turning to face her father. "That proves he's on the level! Frank wouldn't steal anything because he likes living here and doesn't want to get kicked out."

"Dad, look what I found," Lucy said as she came back into the room, holding up a newspaper printed on pink paper. On the front page was a photograph of a mysterious woman, her face hidden behind the collar of her fur coat.

4

"A *Police Gazette*!" Dr. Canellan snatched the pink newspaper from Lucy and looked at it with disgust. "Where did you find this?"

"I went down to the basement to see if Frank hid the tea set under his bed," Lucy said, "but I found the newspaper instead."

Dr. Canellan turned to Frank, fuming. "Is this newspaper yours?"

Catherine and Frank quickly exchanged worried looks. Catherine cleared her throat and stepped forward, but before she could say a word, Frank blurted out, "Yes, it's mine."

"You know I don't allow this trash in the house," Dr. Canellan said, shaking the newspaper. "It's filled with stories of murder and robberies."

"If I were you, Doctor," Mrs. O'Boyle said, "I'd be very worried about the bad influence he has on the girls."

Dr. Canellan frowned and turned to Frank. "I'm very disappointed in you. Go down to the basement and wait there until I decide what to do."

"Yes, sir." Frank walked out of the room with his head down. As he passed Lucy, she stuck her tongue out at him.

Not far from Jamal's house, thirteen-year-old Alex Fernandez struggled across the playground on his new in-line skates. He was feeling proud of himself for staying up when he heard someone shouting his name.

Alex lost his concentration and slipped, landing in the sandbox. He looked up to see his younger sister, Gaby, smiling down at him.

"Ow! See what you made me do?" he said, scowling up at her.

Gaby laughed. "Don't blame me. You're the one who begged Papa to buy those blades for your birthday, even though you don't know how to use them."

"I was doing fine until you snuck up behind me," Alex growled. He struggled to get out of the sandbox, but he tripped and fell again. Gaby laughed even harder.

"Don't you have anything better to do?" Alex snapped.

"Yeah," Gaby said, "I'm going to a rally."

"A rally?" Alex's eyes lit up. "Is Ghostwriter back?"

"No. Here, I brought you this." Gaby tossed Alex his Ghostwriter pen on a string and put her own around her neck. "Jamal and Lenni called on the phone. They think it's time the team got together and made a case out of finding Ghostwriter. The rally is at Jamal's right now. Come on!" Gaby turned and headed out of the park.

"Uh, Gaby?" Alex said quietly. "I could use

some help." Gaby walked back slowly with a big grin on her face. Alex held out his hand. Gaby grabbed it and pulled him out of the sandbox.

"No sweat, Roller Boy. Grab my shoulders and hold on," she said. They took off for Jamal's.

In the basement of the Canellan house, Frank wrote in his diary:

Catherine is the only one who believes me.

He didn't hear Catherine as she opened the door to the basement, quietly closed it behind her, and tiptoed down the stairs and over to Frank's bed.

"You shouldn't be down here!" Frank said, startled to find her standing over him. He snapped his diary shut and put it on the bed. "You'll be in a mess of trouble if you get caught."

"I don't care," Catherine said. She looked curiously at the diary. "What were you doing?"

"I was writing down all the terrible things that happened today," Frank said miserably.

"Why?" asked Catherine.

Frank shrugged. "It helps me figure things out."

"I . . . I want to thank you," Catherine said nervously.

"For what?"

"For not squealing about the *Police Gazette*," Catherine said. "Father would blow his stack if he knew it was mine."

"I may as well take the rap," Frank said. "I'm getting kicked out anyway."

"If only there was a way we could prove you didn't steal the tea set," Catherine said with a sigh.

"Yeah, but how?" Frank asked.

"I don't know exactly." Catherine began to pace. Suddenly she stopped, her eyes wide. "How about all those crime stories I read in the *Police Gazette* and the way the cops track down the gangsters? We can do the same thing!"

"Forget it," Frank said. "A mug like me is always catching the heat. I shoulda known I'd be kicked out sooner or later."

Suddenly Catherine saw that Frank's diary was glowing. "Frank, look!" she shouted, pointing to the diary. It glowed brighter and brighter. "What is it?"

Frank stared at the diary in shock. "Beats me," he finally whispered.

"Let's get out of here!" Catherine cried. She ran for the stairs.

"Watch out!" Frank yelled. Catherine turned around and gasped when she saw what Frank was staring at. Glowing letters from his diary were floating up from the pages and hanging in the air.

Hello, Catherine and Frank.
I'm here to help.

Catherine backed away cautiously, not taking her eyes off the floating words. "How does it know our names?"

"Maybe it's a leprechaun!" Frank said.

"Whatever it is, it's giving me the heebie-jeebies!" Just then the words started to swirl and move again.

"Watch out!" Catherine cried as she grabbed Frank's hand and pulled him into a crouch under the basement stairs. They watched as the words zoomed into Frank's diary and right back out again with another message.

Don't be afraid. Write to me.

Frank took a deep breath and started to crawl toward his diary. Catherine grabbed his arm. "Be careful. Who knows what might happen if you try to write to that thing," she said.

"I want to see," Frank said as he pulled his arm away and crawled to the bed. He picked up a pencil and wrote,

What are you?

Frank held his breath as a ball of bright light streaked across the words he had just written. The light swirled and scrambled letters from the diary, then lifted a new message into the air.

My friends call me Ghostwriter.

"Ghostwriter!" Frank and Catherine shrieked at the same time. Catherine scrambled out from under the stairs and stood close to Frank. "There's no such thing as ghosts, right?" she asked him.

Frank didn't answer as he reached up toward the floating words. When he tried to touch the letters, his hand went right through them. The letters began to spin, then flew down to Frank's bed. "Gee whiz! It's in my diary!" Frank grabbed the diary and slammed it shut. "I got it!" he said triumphantly.

Catherine sighed and began to relax—until she heard a voice calling from upstairs.

"Catherine! Where are you?"

"Oh, no!" Catherine gave Frank a worried look. "Lucy's coming."

"You'd better beat it back to your room before she finds you down here."

Catherine headed for the stairs, but turned back. "What about the ghost?"

"You get rid of Lucy," Frank said, waving her up the stairs. "I'll meet you in your room in a few minutes."

"I'll be waiting!" Catherine said as she dashed up the stairs.

Chapter 2

In Jamal's room, Lenni, Gaby, Alex, and Tina Nguyen listened closely as Jamal started the rally. "What we have to do is find out where Ghostwriter is and get him to come back."

"How?" Tina asked.

"Well, let's think about the last time we saw him," Lenni said. "We were at my place, remember?"

"Yeah," Gaby answered. "What exactly did he say?"

They all tried to remember exactly what had happened when they'd been in Lenni's loft two weeks earlier. They'd been gathered around

Lenni's computer when Ghostwriter typed a message.

> I don't want to go, but this is serious.

"What could be so serious?" Alex had asked. Then Ghostwriter had typed a new message on the screen.

> You would help if you were in my place.

"Of course we would help someone in trouble," Lenni had said. "That's what the Ghostwriter Team is all about."

Then Jamal had asked Ghostwriter if he was coming back, and the rest of the team had held their breath as they waited for Ghostwriter's response.

> I hope I can.

Everyone had watched as Ghostwriter flew out of the screen and left his final message:

> Good-bye, Team.

Now the team sat silently for a moment, remembering how Ghostwriter's final message of two weeks ago had hung in the air.

"So, we know Ghostwriter went to help someone," Jamal finally said, bringing them all back to the present.

"Yeah, whoever it is must be in trouble," Alex said. "I mean, Ghostwriter wouldn't have left if it wasn't an important case. And he's been gone for two weeks!"

"Maybe he's not back because he hasn't solved the case yet," Tina said. "But if we could get him to let us help him solve it, he might come back."

"Yeah, we're still a team!" Jamal said, his brown eyes shining. "We can help Ghostwriter by looking for clues that he can't see because they aren't written down."

"And we can interview suspects and write down what they say," Tina added as Jamal's enthusiasm began to spread.

"We can make a casebook so he can keep track of everything," Gaby said.

Jamal grabbed a bunch of colored markers and notepaper. He passed them out to the rest of the team. "We've got to convince Ghostwriter that he needs the team. Let's all write messages telling him how we want to help!"

Catherine was startled when she saw Frank climbing into her room through the window. She hurried over to help pull him in. "You shouldn't

13

climb up the side of the house. That's how you broke your leg last year."

"I had to get up here without anyone seeing me," Frank said, puffing from the climb. He reached inside his shirt, pulled out his diary, and walked quickly toward Catherine's writing table.

Catherine followed close behind. "What about the Ghostwriter? Is he still in there?"

"I think so." Frank sat down at the desk and cautiously opened the diary.

"Ghostwriter," Catherine said as she leaned close to the diary, "are you in there?" She waited for a moment, expecting the diary to start glowing again, but nothing happened.

Frank looked up at Catherine and said, "It told us to write to it, remember?" He took a pencil out of his shirt pocket and turned to a clean page. "What should I say?"

Catherine thought for a moment. "Ask if it knows who stole my mother's tea set. If we find the thief and the tea set, we'll be sitting pretty!"

"Hey, yeah!" Frank agreed as he started to write:

Do you know who stole the tea set?

A glowing ball of light darted across the letters Frank had just written.

"He's back!" Frank shouted.

Catherine stared wide-eyed at the diary as

14

Ghostwriter moved letters around on the page and gathered new ones from other pages of the diary. When the letters finally stopped moving, Ghostwriter's message was clear.

I know Frank is innocent.

"Yes!" Frank exclaimed. "If Ghostwriter tells your father I'm innocent, then he'll believe in me, too."

"Then we won't have to worry about you being kicked out into the streets," Catherine chimed in, clapping her hands.

Frank turned the page and wrote his request to Ghostwriter:

Will you tell Dr. Canellan I didn't do it?

As they waited for Ghostwriter to respond, Frank began to smile. "If Ghostwriter clears my name, Mrs. O'Boyle will have to take back all the bad things she said about me."

New letters glowed into focus.

Dr. Canellan can't see me.

"Oh, no," Catherine said. "Maybe we're the only ones who can see him."

"But he said his friends call him Ghostwriter," Frank said, puzzled. "If he has friends, they must be able to see him, too." Frank turned back to the diary and began writing furiously:

Can anyone else see you?

Ghostwriter read Frank's question and scrambled letters to respond:

Jamal, Lenni, Alex, Gaby, and Tina

Frank and Catherine looked at each other, confused. "Those must be the names of his friends," Frank said.

"Find out where they are," Catherine said. "If they can help us, we can cover the city looking for the bum who stole the tea set. I can't wait to meet them!"

Frank wrote:

Where can we find them?

In this room, Ghostwriter responded.

Frank and Catherine looked at each other again. "How can they be in this room if we can't see them?" Frank asked.

She and Frank looked at each other, and they both felt chills run up and down their spines.

"Maybe Ghostwriter's friends are ghosts, too!" Catherine said.

The Ghostwriter Team was spread out around Jamal's room, busily writing messages to persuade Ghostwriter to come back.

"Hey, you guys, I wrote a poem. Listen." Gaby stood up and read from her piece of paper.

Ghostwriter, Ghostwriter, where can you be?
Across the ocean, or in a tree?
Ghostwriter, Ghostwriter, I miss you so much.
Send me a message and keep in touch.

Gaby smiled with pride as she looked up from the poem. The other members of the team just stared at her. "Well? What do you think?" she asked.

"Ummm . . . ," Lenni said, trying to be kind. "It's a nice poem, Gaby . . ."

"Yeah, but it's not exactly what we want to say," Jamal added.

Tina walked over to Gaby and put a hand on her shoulder as she tried to explain what was wrong. "We want to let Ghostwriter know how we can help him with the case he's on. So he can come home for good."

"Like this," Lenni said. She put her paper on Jamal's desk so that everyone could see it.

> *Ghostwriter, we can help by being your eyes and ears on the case. We can write all the clues you can't see or hear.*

"That's good, Lenni," Alex said as he stood up to read what he had written:

> *Ghostwriter, the team can be your voice. We'll interview suspects and witnesses for you.*

Alex put his paper down on Jamal's desk next to Lenni's.

"I get it now," Gaby said as she tried to think up a new poem. "How's this? 'Ghostwriter, Ghostwriter, don't stay away. . . . We can write to your friends . . . and save the day!'"

"Yeah!" Jamal cheered.

"I'll write it down," Gaby said, and went back to work.

"Look!" cried Tina, pointing at Lenni's and Alex's papers on Jamal's desk. A very faint yellow glow was moving along the edges of the papers.

Jamal moved in for a closer look. "Ghostwriter?" he said uncertainly.

"What's wrong with him?" Lenni cried. "We can hardly see him."

"The words!" Tina said. "He's connecting to the words in Lenni's and Alex's messages. Let's stack all our messages together. That may bring Ghostwriter back."

"Here!" said Jamal as he put his message on top of Lenni's and Alex's. As soon as his message was with the others, the glow got a little brighter.

"I'm done!" Gaby said, and raced to the desk to add her message to the pile.

They all watched anxiously as Ghostwriter glowed a little more brightly, then began to flicker again.

"Come on, Ghostwriter," Jamal pleaded. "Come back to us!"

"Jamal? Lenni?" Catherine called as she searched under her bed. "Nope, they're not under here." She went back over to the desk, where Frank was writing in the diary to Ghostwriter:

Are your friends ghosts, too?

Ghostwriter's glow zoomed over Frank's question and began to scramble letters to answer him. Suddenly Ghostwriter started spinning faster and faster, like a glowing tornado, until he disappeared into Frank's diary with a blinding flash of light. Frank and Catherine covered their eyes.

They slowly brought their hands down and looked at the diary. There was no trace of Ghostwriter.

"He disappeared!" cried Frank.

"Where'd he go?" Catherine asked.

"I don't know," Frank said, frowning. "But what if he doesn't come back?"

Jamal, Tina, Lenni, Gaby, and Alex stood around the desk watching the glow on their messages get brighter and stronger. "Our words are starting to get through!" said Tina.

At that moment a blinding flash of light exploded out of the pile of messages. Then Ghostwriter was swirling in and out and all around the pile of messages the team had written to him.

"He's back!" Gaby shouted.

The whole team cheered as they watched their glowing friend streak across the room and into Jamal's computer. They all rushed toward the screen to see what Ghostwriter had to say.

Hello, Team!
I'm glad you want to help.

Jamal sat down at the keyboard and began to type:

We missed you! Where have you been?

Ghostwriter quickly responded:

Helping Frank and Catherine

"Frank and Catherine?" Alex said, baffled. "Who are they?"

"They must be the ones in trouble," Lenni said as Jamal typed again:

How can we help you?

Ghostwriter answered:

Prove that Frank is not a thief.

The team members looked at each other, puzzled. How could they prove Frank was not a thief if they didn't know who he was or even where he was?

"Jamal," Tina said, "find out where Frank and Catherine are so we can meet them and get on the case."

Jamal typed:

Where are Frank and Catherine?

Ghostwriter responded:

In this room

"Huh?" said Jamal. "How can they be in my room?"

"He must've made a mistake," Alex said with concern. "Ghostwriter's been gone a long time and he might be . . . you know, confused."

"I have another idea," Tina said. "Ask Ghostwriter to read words near Catherine and Frank. That could help us find them."

Jamal typed:

Please read words near Frank and Catherine.

The team watched as Ghostwriter swirled faster and faster around the screen and then disappeared with a flash of light.

Frank and Catherine paced back and forth in front of the diary, waiting for Ghostwriter to return. They began to panic when they heard Dr. Canellan calling from the hall. "Frank! Frank, are you up here?"

"I gotta scram!" Frank whispered. He dashed to the window and started to climb out, but it was too late. The door banged opened, and in marched Lucy and Mrs. O'Boyle, followed by Dr. Canellan.

"I told you he'd be in here!" Lucy shouted, pointing at Frank.

"Frank, come back in here right now before you fall," Dr. Canellan demanded.

Frank slowly climbed back into the room and turned around, red-faced. At that exact moment a flash of light filled the room and Ghostwriter flew out of Frank's diary. Frank and Catherine stared openmouthed as Ghostwriter raced around the room collecting information to take back to the team.

"Frank. Frank!" Dr. Canellan snapped. But Frank was so caught up in watching Ghostwriter that he didn't respond.

"Frank!" Dr. Canellan snapped again. Dr. Canellan, Lucy, and Mrs. O'Boyle couldn't see Ghostwriter, so they didn't notice when he disappeared into a framed newspaper headline that hung on Catherine's wall.

"The boy is hopeless," Mrs. O'Boyle declared. "He steals, breaks the rules, and doesn't listen to a word you say."

Frank spun around. "Why don't you clam up, Crabapple Annie!" he yelled at Mrs. O'Boyle.

"How dare you!" cried Mrs. O'Boyle.

"Frank!" shouted Dr. Canellan, shocked at the boy's outburst.

"She's always beatin' her gums against me!" Frank spat out, too angry to be worried about the consequences. "If the moon fell out of the sky, she'd find a way to blame me for that, too!"

"How much more proof do you need, Dr. Canellan?" Mrs. O'Boyle demanded. "The boy is a hooligan. He belongs in the Home for Wayward Boys with all the other riffraff."

Dr. Canellan tried to calm the furious housekeeper. "Mrs. O'Boyle, please, we can settle this—"

"Well, you'll have to settle it without me, Doctor," Mrs. O'Boyle announced. "I won't live or work in a house with a guttersnipe like him." She glared at Frank. "If he stays, I go!"

Mrs. O'Boyle put her hands on her hips and waited for Dr. Canellan to order Frank out. But the doctor was silent. Finally Mrs. O'Boyle stormed out of the room.

"No! Father, don't let Mrs. O'Boyle leave us!" Lucy pleaded. She ran out of the room after the housekeeper.

Dr. Canellan took a deep breath and looked out the window. Catherine looked across the room and noticed Ghostwriter flying from the framed newspaper toward Frank's diary. She nudged Frank, and he saw Ghostwriter, too. Ghostwriter swirled above the diary faster and faster and then disappeared with a flash.

Frank and Catherine glanced at each other. It looked as if their hopes of writing to Ghostwriter were dashed. Frank walked slowly to the desk and closed the diary.

Dr. Canellan turned back from the window. "Frank," he said sadly, "you've left me no choice. I can't let you go on disrupting this household. I've thought about it and I'll go to the Home for Wayward Boys tomorrow and find out if they'll take you in."

Frank grabbed his diary and ran out of the room. Catherine turned to her father with tears in her eyes. "Father, no, please! Frank is innocent. That's why he got so angry. Please don't send him away!"

Chapter 3

've started a casebook," Jamal announced to Lenni, Alex, Gaby, and Tina as they waited for Ghostwriter to return. "But this is all we've got."

Frank and Catherine
Who are they?
Where are they?
—In this room?

"If they can see Ghostwriter," Alex wondered aloud, "does that mean they'll be on our team?"

"Why not?" Tina said. "If Ghostwriter writes to them, they must be okay."

Suddenly a yellow ball of light flew into the room. Lenni jumped out of her seat. "He's back!"

Jamal grabbed his casebook, and the team crowded around the computer, anxious to see the clues Ghostwriter had brought back for them. Ghostwriter started typing:

Amelia Earhart Flies Monoplane to England

"England!" shouted Alex. "Is that where Frank and Catherine live?"

"Maybe," Gaby said, and shrugged.

Lenni concentrated on Ghostwriter's clue. "Amelia Earhart was a famous airplane pilot. I read a book about her. I still have it at home."

"Hey, guys," Jamal said, pointing to the computer. "We're getting more clues." They all turned to the screen and read the next clue:

4,000 Athletes Compete in the Ninth Olympic Games

"That's weird," Alex said. "The summer games this year are going to be the twenty-sixth." Jamal shrugged and quickly copied down the message as Ghostwriter gave them another clue.

West End Blues Louis Armstrong and the Hot Five

"Louis Armstrong?" Gaby asked. "Who's he?"

"Just one of the most famous jazz musicians who ever lived, dummy," Alex said to his little sister.

"Everyone called him Satchmo," Jamal told Gaby in a gentle voice. "He played the trumpet and sang." Jamal pretended to play a trumpet and did a gravelly-voiced impersonation of Louis Armstrong singing.

"But what about the West End Blues?" Alex asked. "And who are the Hot Five?"

"Hey, you guys, look at Ghostwriter!" Tina said, pointing at the screen. "What's wrong with him?" On the computer screen, Ghostwriter's words were blinking off and on and fading.

"Maybe he's tired," Alex said. "Can a ghost get tired?"

"I don't know, but I guess we're going to have to figure out what these clues mean on our own," Jamal said. "We can't let Ghostwriter down."

"I'll go home and get my Amelia Earhart book," Lenni volunteered.

"Cool," said Jamal. "I'll go to the library and see what I can find out about the West End Blues and the Hot Five."

"I'll go with you," said Gaby. "I can look up the ninth Olympics."

Alex knew he wouldn't be allowed inside the library wearing Rollerblades. He decided to stay in Jamal's room to see if he could get more information about Frank and Catherine from Ghostwriter. Tina had to go with her parents to visit her aunt, who had just had a baby. Alex promised to call her later that evening to fill her in on the case.

"Okay," said Jamal. "We all know what we have to do. Let's get moving and meet back here with whatever we find out!"

Jamal and Gaby dashed up the stone steps of the Carroll Street Library. They had been going to the small neighborhood branch ever since they could remember. It wasn't as new as some of the other libraries in Brooklyn, and it didn't have computers like the library in Jamal's school, but they loved its familiar stacks and comfortable reading chairs.

Inside, Jamal pointed to the shelves that held the encyclopedias. "I'm gonna look up Louis Armstrong," he told Gaby.

"Okay," Gaby said, strolling over to the librarian's desk. When the librarian looked up with a smile, Gaby asked where she could find information about the ninth Olympics. The librarian told Gaby to check the computer catalog under the heading "Olympics" and search through the list of books. Gaby thanked the librarian and headed for the computers.

Ten minutes later, Jamal and Gaby had the information they needed.

"The ninth Olympic Games"—Gaby read aloud to Jamal—"were played in Amsterdam, the Netherlands, in 1928."

"Great! I found some stuff about the West End Blues and the Hot Five. Let's get back to my room and see what Lenni and Alex have come up with."

Back in Jamal's room, Lenni and Alex listened as Jamal explained that the Hot Five was Louis Armstrong's first jazz band.

"What about the West End Blues?" Lenni asked.

Jamal checked the notes he had copied into his casebook. "'West End Blues' was one of the songs they recorded in 1928."

"What about Amelia Earhart?" Alex asked Lenni.

Lenni picked up her paperback book on Amelia Earhart. "She was an airplane pilot who tried to fly around the world in 1937 and disappeared. No one ever saw her again."

Jamal checked his casebook. "But the clue Ghostwriter gave us says she flew a monoplane to England."

"Oh, yeah," Lenni said, reopening her book. "That was her first flight across the ocean. She flew in a monoplane to England in 1928."

"Nineteen twenty-eight!" Jamal said with excitement as he checked the facts in the casebook. "All of these things happened in 1928!"

"Maybe Frank and Catherine are in a museum," Gaby said.

"Or they could be reading a lot of old newspapers from 1928," Lenni guessed.

"But Ghostwriter said they were in this room," Jamal said.

Alex looked around the room. "Well, they aren't here *now*."

"But what if they *were* here *then*?" Jamal said. The whole team looked at him as if he were crazy. "What if Frank and Catherine lived in this house in 1928?"

"Say what?" blurted out Alex.

"That's impossible," Lenni said. "Unless . . ."

Lenni, Jamal, Alex, and Gaby looked at each other, astonished. Finally Jamal said what they were all thinking. "Ghostwriter can travel through time!"

They all looked at the computer. A weak light glowed faintly at the bottom of the screen.

"Ghostwriter never told us he could travel through time," Gaby said.

"Do you think he knows?" Lenni asked.

"He sure doesn't know that Frank and Catherine are in 1928. Look at the way his glow is getting weak," Alex said. "Looks like he has hardly enough energy to stay on the screen. He probably has to fly at triple supersonic speed to go back in time. It's not as easy as just cruising around the neighborhood, that's for sure!"

Gaby sat at the computer keyboard. "I'll tell Ghostwriter what we found out," she said, and started typing.

Lenni plopped into Jamal's beanbag chair. "Nineteen twenty-eight! Man, that sure was a long, long, time ago," she said quietly.

"Yeah," Alex agreed. "My parents weren't even born yet."

"Neither was my grandma," Jamal added.

"Can you imagine?" Lenni asked. "No CDs, no cassettes."

"Wow," Alex said. "No video games . . . no television . . ."

"No *us*!" said Jamal. "Now *that's* a scary thought."

Lenni crawled out of the beanbag chair and looked over Gaby's shoulder at the computer screen. "I wonder what's so important that Ghostwriter has to help kids who lived in this house"— Lenni quickly counted in her head—"sixty-eight years ago!"

Gaby had finished typing her message to Ghostwriter telling him that he'd been traveling back through time to 1928. Ghostwriter read the message and answered:

Astounding!
No wonder I'm so tired!

"While you guys were at the library," Alex reported to the team, "Ghostwriter told me that Frank is being accused of stealing a silver tea set, but he's innocent. I don't see why that's important enough to make Ghostwriter go back in time."

"I'll ask him," Gaby said as she started typing.

Why is this case so important to you?

Helping Frank will save our team.

"How?" Gaby typed.

"?" was Ghostwriter's response.

"He doesn't know," said Jamal.

Lenni shook her head. "This is our strangest case yet!" Gaby started typing again.

What can we do to help Frank and Catherine?

Ghostwriter read the question and typed his response:

Teach them how to solve a case.

"Hey, that's right!" Jamal exclaimed. "If we teach them how we solve cases, then they can prove Frank is innocent."

"I never thought about *how* we do what we do," Lenni said.

"Yeah, it just comes naturally to us," Gaby said, and shrugged.

Alex laughed. "That's because you love sticking your nose into everybody's business."

Jamal and Lenni laughed. Gaby rolled her eyes at her big brother. She was used to his lame jokes at her expense.

Jamal noticed that it was getting late. "Let's meet back here first thing tomorrow," he said. "Then we'll try to figure out how we do the detective 'thang.'"

After Lenni, Alex, and Gaby had left, Jamal noticed Ghostwriter. He was still at the bottom of the computer screen, glowing very faintly. Jamal walked over to the screen and said, "Get some rest, Ghostwriter." He turned off the computer, and the screen went black.

Chapter 4

In the basement of the Canellan house, Frank, his face streaked with tears, was lying across his bed and staring at a poster on the wall. The poster had a picture of a train with the words *Twentieth Century* written under it.

Frank was roused from his daydream when he heard footsteps. Dr. Canellan walked down the stairs carrying a dinner tray. "I thought you might be hungry," he said, setting the tray on a table near the bed. "You know, everyone thought I was crazy for letting a boy move in with my family after I had caught him robbing my house." Dr. Canellan sat on the edge of the bed. "But I knew you were special, Frank. The way you fought to survive, alone, with no parents. The way you talked so passionately about wanting to become a doctor when you grew up. Even the amazement on your face when I told you I'd *help* you reach your goal. I was so sure I was doing the right thing. I wanted you to be a part of this family. But we agreed that if you stole again you'd have to leave."

"But I didn't swipe the tea set," Frank protested.

"I wish I could believe you," Dr. Canellan said.

"What if I could prove it to you?" Frank asked. "Would you still kick me out?"

"I wish you *could* prove it to me, Frank." Dr. Canellan looked at the boy closely. "If you did that, we could start all over. But as it stands now— the tea set, bringing the *Police Gazette* into the house, climbing in and out of windows, and yelling at Mrs. O'Boyle—I'm not so sure you really belong here."

Frank turned away from Dr. Canellan and buried his face in his pillow. Dr. Canellan looked at the boy sadly, then got up and slowly climbed the stairs.

When Frank heard the door at the top of the stairs close, he stood on the bed. He carefully pulled a loose brick out of the wall, then reached in and brought out a stack of letters. The letters were old and yellowed. The address on the front of the envelopes read:

Mrs. Elizabeth Flynn
10 Bowery Lane
Brooklyn, New York

He lay back down on his bed and gently opened the first envelope.

A few hours later, sunlight streamed through the basement window. Catherine, carrying her book bag, tiptoed down the stairs.

Frank was sound asleep on his bed. The food on the table was untouched. Frank was fully dressed and surrounded by the old letters he had been reading when he fell asleep.

"Frank, wake up," Catherine whispered. "It's morning."

"Hi, Catherine," Frank said sleepily.

Catherine noticed the letters on the bed. "Who are these letters from?" she asked.

"These are the last letters my mother ever got from my father," Frank said as he began to gather the letters and carefully put them back into their envelopes. "He used to write to her every day when he went away to find work. When the letters stopped coming, we didn't know if he was alive or dead."

"I'm sorry," Catherine said as she sat down on the bed next to him. She had never heard him talk about his family before.

"From that time on, my mother got sadder and

sadder," Frank went on. "She had to work day and night to take care of us. I think that's why her heart got sick, and she died. If we had any money, she could have gone to a doctor, and she'd probably still be alive. That's why I wanted to become a doctor so much."

"You will become a doctor, Frank," Catherine insisted.

"That's a bunch of baloney and you know it!" Frank said.

"You can give up if you like, Frank Flynn. But I know you're innocent, and I'm going to prove it."

"How's that?" Frank asked doubtfully.

"Ghostwriter wants to help us," Catherine insisted.

"Has he come back?"

"No."

"Then we're sunk," Frank concluded.

"Now that's baloney!" Catherine argued as she stood up and headed for the stairs. "And if I have to, I'll find the thief by myself."

Frank got up and followed Catherine. "Where are you going?"

Catherine stopped on the stairs and turned back to Frank, her eyes flashing with excitement. "I overheard Mrs. O'Boyle and the housekeeper from next door talking about some other burglaries in this neighborhood. Maybe the same thief who broke into those other houses robbed us, too. I'm going to the library to see what I can find in last week's newspapers and *Police Gazette*. I'll be back as soon as I can."

Frank thought for a moment, then called out to Catherine before she got to the top of the stairs. "Wait for me on the corner. I'm coming with you."

"But Frank, you're not supposed to leave the basement," Catherine warned. "You'll get into more hot water."

"Your father's throwing me out anyway." Frank shrugged. "What have I got to lose? Now go!"

Frank watched as Catherine ran up the stairs and out the door. When she was gone, he went back to his bed and picked up the letters from his father. He stacked them neatly, then put them in the hiding place in the wall above the bed.

At the top of the stairs, Lucy peeked through the slightly opened door. She watched Frank as he removed the brick and put the letters into the hole. As Frank pushed the brick into place, Lucy smiled to herself.

Frank quickly tucked in his shirt, grabbed his cap, and headed for the stairs. Lucy darted out of sight.

Frank paused halfway up the stairs. What if Mrs. O'Boyle saw him? He decided to climb through the basement window near the stairs. Frank put his foot on the banister to give himself a boost, opened the window, and crawled out to the alley.

As soon as Frank was gone, Lucy crept into the basement. She went straight to the wall behind Frank's bed and ran her hands along it until she found the loose brick. Her heart was beating fast as she pulled the brick out of the wall. She reached in and yanked out the stack of letters, letting them tumble to the floor. She picked one up and began to read.

Jamal stood in his basement staring at the dozens of dusty old boxes that had been shoved under the stairs, into corners, and onto shelves over the years. Lenni, Alex, and Gaby came clattering down the stairs a few minutes later.

"Hey, guys! I was just looking through this stuff to see if I could find anything that belonged to Frank and Catherine," Jamal said. "I mean, they lived here in 1928, so you never know. And my grandma never throws anything away. . . ."

"Any luck?" Lenni asked.

"Not yet," Jamal said as he brushed his hands together to get rid of some of the dust.

"Well, let's get to figuring out how to teach Frank and Catherine to solve a case," Lenni said.

Alex pulled a book out of his pocket and held it

up. "I was looking through *The Young Detective's Handbook* that I got at the book fair. And it seems to me that finding suspects is the most important thing."

"Really?" Lenni asked, not at all convinced. "I think it's keeping track of the evidence. If you don't do that, how are you gonna prove which of the suspects is guilty?"

Jamal chimed in with another point of view. "We have to teach Frank and Catherine how to *think* like detectives. They have to know how to write down clues that might not seem important or that might not seem to fit."

"No, that's not it," Alex argued.

"Uh-uh, I don't think so, either," Lenni said.

"Hey, I know what I'm talking about," Jamal insisted.

Gaby was silent as she watched her teammates bickering. Finally she stepped in. "Hey, hey, what are you guys arguing about? We write *all* that stuff down in the casebook, right?"

"Sure we do," said Lenni. Alex and Jamal nodded.

"Solving a case is like . . ." Gaby closed her eyes, searching for just the right image. "Solving a case is like putting a jigsaw puzzle together! And the casebook is where we keep all the pieces. The most important thing we can teach Frank and Catherine is how to make a casebook. Because that's the best way to start piecing the puzzle."

"Piecing the puzzle?" Jamal asked.

"Yeah," Gaby said, proud of the phrase she had coined. "Like organizing stuff. Getting it together."

"I gotta hand it to you, Gaby," Alex said. "Teaching them to make a casebook makes a lot of sense."

"I told you," Gaby said confidently. "It just comes naturally."

Chapter 5

Catherine and Frank sat at a table in the Carroll Street Library looking in recent newspapers for articles about robberies. The Carroll Street Library was the newest library in Brooklyn, and it had a great periodicals section. It was easy for Catherine and Frank to find back issues of the *Brooklyn Eagle* newspaper and the *Police Gazette.*

"I found something!" Catherine said, looking up from the newspaper she was reading. She turned the paper toward Frank so that he could read along.

SILVER BIRDCAGE FLIES THE COOP!

Mrs. Judith Moreland has reported the theft of a valuable antique silver birdcage and two lovebirds. Police suspect there may be a connection to two other recent burglaries in Brooklyn. In each case, valuable items made of silver have been reported stolen. Police have no leads yet.

"Jeepers," Frank said as he finished reading the article. "The police aren't doing any better than we are."

"But we can show this article to my father and Mrs. O'Boyle," Catherine said hopefully. "When they read it, they'll realize you're innocent."

"But what if they think I stole the silver birdcage and robbed the other houses, too?" Frank asked. "Especially Mrs. O'Boyle. She'd probably turn me in to the police!"

"You're right. We can't take that chance," Catherine said. She picked up another newspaper and passed it to Frank. "Keep looking for more articles about silver being stolen. Maybe the police have found some clues since this was written."

Jamal sat at his computer, with Lenni, Alex, and Gaby surrounding him.

"First we should explain why keeping a casebook is important," Jamal said.

Lenni thought for a moment. "The casebook is where you keep track of clues."

"So you can see what information fits together and solve the case," added Alex.

"Then you write down all the suspects, evidence, and other stuff that might be important," Gaby said.

"We can't just say it like that," Alex insisted. "We have to make these instructions as clear as we can so that Catherine and Frank will be able to make their own casebook."

"Yeah," Lenni agreed. "We have to use words that'll let them picture exactly what we mean."

"Okay, okay, I get it," Gaby grumbled. "First they have to make a suspects list. We make a separate page for each suspect."

"And the evidence against that suspect goes on the same page," Lenni said. "Like, where they were when the crime happened and all the reasons they might have for committing the crime."

"This is great, you guys," Jamal said, typing as fast as he could. "Keep it coming."

"Tell them to make another page to keep track of the other clues," Gaby offered.

Jamal stopped typing and turned to his teammates. "I think we have to explain what 'other clues' are."

"How about this," Lenni volunteered. "Other

clues are all the facts or observations that might be important but don't fit anywhere else."

"But these clues might be useful later on," said Alex.

Jamal finished typing and printed out his work. "If Frank and Catherine follow these instructions, they should be able to solve their case."

"I sure hope so," said Gaby. "Then Ghostwriter can come back to us for good."

When the finished instructions came out of the printer, they all gathered around to check out their work:

How to Solve a Case

1. Make a page for each suspect.

SUSPECT
Who might have done it?

EVIDENCE
Where was suspect?
Why would suspect do it?

2. Make a page for OTHER CLUES.

Write facts that may be
important to help solve the case.

Ghostwriter glowed all over the instructions as he read them. He flew into the computer and typed a message for Jamal, Lenni, Alex, and Gaby:

Good work, Team! Thank you.

"Ghostwriter's not blinking anymore!" Lenni exclaimed.

Gaby smiled. "He's rested and ready to go."

They watched as Ghostwriter swirled around and around the instructions. The ball of light spun faster and faster until it disappeared with a flash.

"Ghostwriter's got a lot of words to carry back to 1928," Jamal said. "I hope he makes it."

In a tunnel filled with swirling newspaper print, Ghostwriter was pulled back in time. The trip was hard, almost like swimming upstream. Ghostwriter was jerked from side to side and sometimes smashed into the sides of the tunnel. But he kept going, because he knew the information he was carrying back to 1928 would somehow save the team in 1996.

Catherine and Frank were still in the library busily searching through recent newspapers. Suddenly the *Brooklyn Eagle* newspaper Frank was reading began to glow with a warm light, and letters began to spin around. "Ghostwriter!" Frank shouted.

Catherine immediately looked up from the *Po-*

lice Gazette she was reading and shouted, "He's back!"

"Shhh!" hissed a short, chubby man at the table next to Frank and Catherine.

"Sorry," Catherine apologized. She picked up her book bag and went around to Frank's side of the table to get a better look at Ghostwriter's message.

Frank watched wide-eyed as the spinning letters began to settle into new words. "This must be a message from Ghostwriter's friends."

Catherine was reading the message almost as quickly as the words were forming. "We have to make a casebook to keep track of suspects, evidence, and other clues." Catherine opened her book bag and took out a composition notebook. She started writing fast. "I'm going to get this down before Ghostwriter disappears again," she said.

When Catherine finished copying the message, she turned to Frank, eager to start a casebook. "So, who's our first suspect?"

Frank thought for a moment, then shouted, "Mrs. O'Boyle!"

Catherine was surprised. "Why?" she asked. "What kind of evidence do we have against her?"

"She was at the house when the tea set was stolen," Frank replied.

Catherine was still unsure. "But why would she steal it?"

"Because she wants to frame me," Frank said, his eyes flashing with resentment. "You know, make it look like I did it so your father will kick me out of the house."

Catherine had to admit that Mrs. O'Boyle had had it in for Frank ever since he moved into the Canellan house a year ago.

Catherine wrote:

SUSPECT
Mrs. O'Boyle
EVIDENCE
in the house
wants Frank thrown out

"Well, we've got our first suspect," Catherine said triumphantly.

"*Hotchacha!*" whooped Frank. The short, fat man gave them a dirty look. "I didn't believe we could do this, but now I'm starting to feel like a real detective," Frank whispered.

Catherine looked down at the casebook. "Ghostwriter's friends must be experts at solving cases," she said.

"I wonder why they didn't just come help us themselves," said Frank.

"Maybe they can't," offered Catherine. "Let's ask Ghostwriter to thank them for us." She quickly turned to another page in the casebook and wrote:

Ghostwriter, please thank your friends for helping us.

Ghostwriter took a long time to rearrange enough letters to respond to Frank and Catherine:

```
I must rest before I return to
1996.
```

Frank and Catherine stared at the page, then looked at each other in amazement. "Nineteen ninety-six!" Catherine exclaimed.

"Ghostwriter's friends live in the future?" Frank asked. "No, that's impossible! I don't believe it!"

Catherine watched as the letters Ghostwriter had used to write to them swirled back into place and the glow disappeared from the casebook. "If someone had told us about Ghostwriter before we met him, we wouldn't have believed that either, would we?"

"No, but—"

"Frank, don't you see? Something wonderful is happening," Catherine said, her eyes filled with excitement. "For some reason, there are people in the future trying to help us. We should be grateful."

Frank thought it over for a moment. "I guess you're right. But 1996! Why, I'd be . . . really, really old!"

"Me too," Catherine said as she began to imagine what she would be like in the future. "I'd probably have lots and lots of gray hair."

"And we'd both have to use canes to help us walk!" Frank said. "Boy, this is awfully strange!"

"And awfully exciting!" Catherine giggled as she turned to the next blank page in her casebook. "Who's our next suspect?"

"Lucy!" Frank blurted out immediately.

"Lucy?" Catherine asked, surprised. "But she's my sister."

"She was also in the house when the tea set was stolen," Frank pointed out. "And she doesn't like me, so she has a reason to want to frame me."

"Yeah, I guess you're right. I'll put her down." Catherine felt a twinge of guilt as she added her sister to the suspects list.

SUSPECT
Lucy Canellan
EVIDENCE
in the house
dislikes Frank

When Catherine finished writing, she closed her casebook. "Now we should interview our suspects to try to find out if they're guilty or if they have any other information."

"But what about the silver burglaries we read about in the newspaper?" asked Frank.

"We don't know who's behind those thefts."

"But it might be important," Frank said. "We should write that stuff down in the 'other clues' section."

Catherine opened the casebook and started writing.

OTHER CLUES
silver stolen from 2 houses in Brooklyn

Frank smiled proudly as he looked at the casebook. "Ghostwriter's friends were right. This is a keen way to keep track of the case."

"Let's go home," Catherine said. "You have to get back in the basement before someone discovers you're missing. I'll interview Mrs. O'Boyle and Lucy."

"To find out if they set me up?"

"Yeah, but they might also lead us to more suspects and clues." Catherine stuffed the casebook into her book bag and stood up. "Let's go, gumshoe!"

Frank lifted his foot so that he could check the bottom of his shoe. "Hey, I don't have any gum on my shoe."

Catherine laughed. "*Gumshoe* is another word for detective. I learned it from reading the *Police Gazette.*"

"Oh," Frank said as he picked up his cap and followed Catherine out of the library. "Gumshoe. I like that. Sounds kinda tough!"

Chapter 6

Alex and Jamal headed back down to Jamal's basement. Alex pulled a large, dust-covered crate from under the stairs. He blew across the top, sending a cloud of dust over Jamal.

"Hey, man, watch what you're doing," Jamal complained between coughs.

Alex laughed. "Sorry, Jamal, but we might as well get everything nice and clean for Grandma CeCe while we're down here."

Just then the basement door opened. The boys looked up to see Grandma CeCe at the top of the stairs. She had her purse and keys in her hand and a serious look on her face. "Jamal, your father's job just called. He's not feeling well, and he wants me to drive over and pick him up."

"What's wrong with him?" Jamal asked, frowning.

"I'm sure it's nothing serious," Grandma CeCe assured him. "He probably has a toothache or something. Lunch is on the table. I'll be back soon."

Grandma CeCe waved and left.

"My dad must be real sick if he can't make it home by himself," Jamal said after she left.

"It's probably no big deal," Alex replied. "Let's go upstairs and eat."

"Yeah, come on," Jamal said as he brushed himself off and headed upstairs.

Catherine was sitting in the living room with the casebook opened on her lap and a fine, silver-colored pen on a string around her neck. She was interviewing Mrs. O'Boyle, who was busily swiping at a chair with a feather duster.

"Was anyone else in the house yesterday before the silver tea set was stolen?" Catherine asked.

"Mr. Izzo, the coal man, made a delivery," Mrs. O'Boyle replied, without looking up from her work. "He had to come through the house to get the key for the coal chute because Frank forgot to unlock it for him."

Catherine quickly added Mr. Izzo to the suspects list. "Anyone else?" she inquired.

"No one," Mrs. O'Boyle answered with a heavy sigh. "But you're crazy if you think Frank didn't steal that tea set. There's no getting around the fact that he's a thief. A leopard can't change his stripes!"

Catherine looked up from writing in the casebook. "Leopards have spots. Zebras have stripes."

"Well," Mrs. O'Boyle retorted haughtily, "whatever they have, they can't change them!"

"Why do you dislike Frank so much?" Catherine asked.

Mrs. O'Boyle stopped dusting and sat on the couch next to Catherine. "I grew up in the slums around hoodlums just like Frank. When I was a little girl, I saw a gang of street boys attack my father for a loaf of bread. My poor Da was hurt so bad he couldn't work anymore. My sisters and I had to leave school and get jobs so our family wouldn't be thrown out into the streets. Those thieving hoodlums ruined my life!" Mrs. O'Boyle's eyes began to fill with tears. She took a lace handkerchief out of her pocket and gently dabbed her eyes.

Catherine had never seen Mrs. O'Boyle cry before. "Are you all right?" she asked, feeling a quick stab of pity for the housekeeper.

"I'm fine," Mrs. O'Boyle responded. "I always get misty when I think of what they did to my dear father."

Catherine moved closer to Mrs. O'Boyle and patted her arm. "I'm sorry that happened to your father, Mrs. O'Boyle, but Frank doesn't do those kinds of things."

"Hrumph!" Mrs. O'Boyle snorted as she stood and started sweeping the feather duster across the coffee table. "So you say." A few feathers fell out of the duster and floated across the table. "Darn that Millard Fillmore Smith! He's a liar and a cheat!" Mrs. O'Boyle said angrily.

"Who are you talking about?" Catherine asked.

"Millard Fillmore Smith, the Ritter Brush man," Mrs. O'Boyle answered testily. "I bought this feather duster from him yesterday."

"Yesterday?" Catherine wondered if he could be another suspect. "What time?"

"Right after I finished the breakfast dishes."

"I thought you said no one else was in the house," Catherine said as she turned to a clean page in the casebook. "Tell me everything that happened while he was here."

Mrs. O'Boyle pointed the feather duster at the sofa. "He sat right there and promised that this feather duster would last a lifetime. And to think he was named after my favorite president!"

As Catherine started to write in her casebook, she said, "He was here before the tea set was stolen, so he's a suspect!"

"Nonsense!" Mrs. O'Boyle chortled as she headed out of the living room. "He's a traveling salesman, not a common thief."

Catherine finished writing in the casebook.

SUSPECT
Millard Fillmore Smith,
Ritter Brush man
EVIDENCE
in the house before theft

Catherine closed the casebook and stood up. *Two more suspects! I've got to report this to Frank,* she thought.

On her way out of the living room, Catherine noticed something on the floor near the breakfront where the silver tea set had been kept. She moved in for a closer look and saw that it was a footprint. She rubbed her finger across it. *It's coal dust,* she thought. *This could be evidence against the coal man!*

Catherine sat on the floor and opened her casebook to Mr. Izzo's page, where she began recording the evidence.

Downstairs, Lucy was so busy reading the letters she had stolen from Frank's hiding place, she nearly jumped out of her skin when she heard him climbing through the basement window. She grabbed up all the scattered letters and raced to the hiding place. She quickly shoved the letters in and replaced the brick.

When Lucy turned to leave, she saw that she had dropped one of the letters on the floor. She snatched it up and hid it behind her back before Frank had climbed all the way through the window and dropped down.

"What are you doing here?" Frank snarled when he saw Lucy.

"None of your beeswax!" Lucy sniffed. She tried to dodge around Frank to get to the staircase, but he blocked her way.

"You really want to get me kicked out of here, don't you?" Frank asked.

"Yes."

"Why?" Frank demanded.

"Because you stole my mother's tea set," Lucy said accusingly.

"I didn't steal it," Frank said. "Besides, you wanted to get rid of me long before that happened. How come?"

"Because since you've been here, Catherine never plays with me anymore," Lucy said. "She spends all her time with you, keeping secrets. When you're gone, she'll want to be my best friend again."

Frank squinted his eyes as he looked at Lucy. "Is that why you stole the tea set and tried to blame it on me? So I'd get kicked out?"

"You can't blame that on me," Lucy said with a smirk. "I'm not a thief like you!" She started toward the stairs, but Frank blocked her way again. Lucy looked at him with cold eyes. "You'd better move before I call Mrs. O'Boyle and tell her you left the house when you weren't supposed to."

Frank bowed his head and stepped aside.

Lucy marched up the stairs confidently, hiding the letter in her folded arms. When she reached the top of the stairs, she turned back and shouted, "I hope my father throws you out tonight!" She slammed the door as hard as she could.

Meanwhile, Catherine was kneeling on the floor of the living room, carefully tracing the footprint into her casebook, when she looked up to see Mrs. O'Boyle and Lucy standing over her.

"What are you doing?" Mrs. O'Boyle demanded.

"Nothing!" Catherine said as she stood up and closed the casebook.

"Lunch will be late," Mrs. O'Boyle said, eyeing her suspiciously. "Lucy and I are off to the butcher shop. We'll be back soon."

"Good-bye, Catherine," Lucy said sweetly. "Make sure Frank stays downstairs in the basement where he belongs." She smiled wickedly as she took Mrs. O'Boyle's hand and followed her out the door.

Catherine ran to the basement door and called for Frank to come upstairs.

Frank entered the living room cautiously. "Where's Mrs. O'Boyle?"

"Don't worry," Catherine said as she grabbed Frank's arm and led him into the living room. "She and Lucy are gone. Look at this."

"What is it?" asked Frank.

Catherine ran her finger over the footprint and held it up for Frank to see. "It's a footprint made of coal dust. I found out that the coal man came into the house before he made his delivery yesterday morning."

"So he's a suspect!" Frank said.

"Right," Catherine replied, looking at Mr. Izzo's page in the casebook. "I wish I knew where we could find him. He's probably somewhere burglarizing another house right now."

"Maybe Ghostwriter can help."

"How?" Catherine asked.

"Well, he can fly around and read things. Maybe he can find the coal wagon by looking for that big sign painted on it. It says Ice and Coal, Izzo Bros."

"Let's give it a try," Catherine said. She set the casebook on the breakfront and started to write to Ghostwriter.

Frank looked around the comfortable living room while he waited for Catherine to finish.

"This sure is a swell joint. I'll bet the Home for Wayward Boys is a cold and ugly place."

"Stop worrying, Frank, we're making progress. Look!" Catherine pointed to the casebook, where she had written:

Ghostwriter, can you find a wagon with Izzo Bros. painted on it?

Ghostwriter read the request and rearranged some letters to respond:

I can try.

Frank and Catherine watched as Ghostwriter flew out of the house.

Catherine reached into her pocket and pulled out another silver pen that she had attached to a string. It was just like the one she was wearing around her neck.

"This is for you to wear so that you'll always be ready to write down anything important to the case."

"Wow, thanks, Catherine," Frank said as he hung the pen around his neck. "I caught Lucy snooping around downstairs. I tried to question her, but she was as cool as a cucumber. She wouldn't admit to anything."

"Did you know there was a Ritter Brush man

here yesterday morning before the tea set was stolen?" Catherine asked.

"No," said Frank. "We should try to find him, too."

"We may not have to if the coal man turns out to be the thief."

Ghostwriter flew back into the room and zoomed onto the casebook with a message:

Cobble St. and Grant Lane

"That must be where the coal truck is," Catherine shouted as she grabbed the casebook. "It's not too far away. Let's skedaddle!"

As Alex continued to search through the dusty boxes in the basement, Jamal sat on the stairs eating a sandwich.

"Hey, look at these!" Alex shouted as he pulled an old newspaper out of one of the boxes. It was printed on pink paper, and the pages were very fragile. "This is a *Police Gazette*. I've seen them in the library. They're full of crime stories and other good junk!"

Jamal had never heard of the *Police Gazette*. Alex told him they were popular a long time ago. He checked the date at the top of the page. The newspaper he was holding had been printed in 1928!

"Maybe it belonged to Frank and Catherine," Jamal said.

"I'll bet it did," Alex said. "Let's see what else we can find."

They went back to their search, more determined than ever.

Chapter 7

Frank and Catherine were crouched behind a car across the street from where the Izzo Bros. coal wagon was parked. They hadn't been waiting long when a tall, burly man walked out of a house and headed for the truck. He was carrying a burlap sack with something bulky in it.

"Why is he coming out of the front of the house?" Catherine asked suspiciously. "The coal chute is in the back."

"And look at that sack he's carrying," Frank whispered. "Maybe he stole something else. You go home," Frank told Catherine as the coal man got into his wagon. "I'm going to get in the back of the wagon and keep an eye on him."

"I'm no Chicken Little!" Catherine protested. "I'm going with you. We're partners on this case, kiddo, and I can do anything you can do. Come on!"

Catherine and Frank ran across the street and leaped into the back of the coal wagon just as it was about to take off. The back of the wagon was full of coal and straw. Frank and Catherine hunkered down to keep out of sight.

Soon the wagon turned into an alley and stopped in front of a warehouse. After waiting a few minutes, Frank peered around the side of the wagon. The driver's seat was empty. "He's gone!" Frank whispered to Catherine.

"Let's see if he left the sack up front," Catherine said.

Frank and Catherine climbed down from the back of the wagon and started creeping toward the front. Suddenly they were grabbed from behind and lifted off the ground. They looked up and saw the snarling coal man staring down at them.

"What are you two following me for?" Mr. Izzo demanded. "What's your beef?"

"Put us down, you big palooka, before I hurt ya!" Frank yelled as he struggled to get away. Mr. Izzo laughed. That made Frank so angry that he socked the coal man in the jaw.

"Ow!" Mr. Izzo cried as he let go of Frank and Catherine and rubbed his jaw. "Jeepers, kid, you pack an awful wallop."

"And there's a lot more where that came from, ya dirty crook!" Frank shouted, puffing out his chest.

"You stole my mother's silver tea set, and probably lots of other things from other houses, too," Catherine cried.

"You kids are cuckoo!" Mr. Izzo yelled. "I been delivering coal on this beat since before you were born. Why would I start lootin' houses all of a sudden?"

"Aw, bushwa!" shouted Frank.

"Yeah, bushwa!" Catherine chimed in.

"You pups are beginning to get on my nerves! I didn't steal nothin'!"

"Then prove it," Frank challenged. "Show us what you got in the sack if you're so innocent."

Mr. Izzo went to the front of the wagon and took the burlap sack off the driver's seat. He reached inside and pulled out a large, round loaf of bread that a customer had given him for lunch.

Frank flushed red with embarrassment. Catherine leaned into him and whispered, "What about the footprint?"

"Hold up your dogs," Frank yelled at Mr. Izzo. "What for?"

"Quit your gripin' and do it!" Frank demanded.

Mr. Izzo muttered to himself as he sat on the side of the wagon and lifted his foot for inspection. Catherine turned to the page with the outline of the footprint that she had traced. She held it up to

Mr. Izzo's foot. Mr. Izzo laughed. His foot was almost twice as large as the footprint in Catherine's notebook.

Catherine and Frank quickly apologized.

"Well, I'll let you kids off only because you're such tough little cusses," Mr. Izzo said. He was chuckling as he disappeared into the warehouse with his loaf of bread.

"Well, that knocks out our number one suspect. Now what do we do?" Frank asked as he sat on the curb.

"Keep looking, that's what," said Catherine.

"Aw, what's the use? We're never gonna catch the thief." Frank clenched his fists and bit his lip trying not to cry, but he couldn't help it. "I ain't going to the Home for Wayward Boys, I tell ya. I'll run away first. I mean it, I'll run away!" Wiping away tears, Frank stood and took off running out of the alley.

Catherine ran after Frank. She finally caught up to him a couple of blocks away. He was sitting on a curb, wiping more tears from his eyes.

"Sorry I cried in front of you," Frank said.

"Everybody has to cry sometimes," Catherine said, sitting down next to him.

"Not where I come from. When you live on the streets, you have to be tough all the time or you won't survive."

"Just because you cry doesn't mean you're not tough," Catherine said. "A tough guy is someone who keeps trying no matter how bad things look. Are you tough enough to keep trying to find out who the real thief is?"

Frank slumped over. He didn't answer.

Catherine stood over Frank and scolded him. "If you run away, Frank Flynn, you're just a coward!"

"Hey, I'm no coward!" Frank protested, sitting up straight.

"Then I guess we'd better get back on the case," Catherine said. She pulled Frank up from the curb. "Come on, we haven't got any time to waste!"

Jamal rushed over to his dad when he appeared on the basement steps. "Hey, Dad, are you all right?"

"Yeah, I'm fine," Reggie Jenkins assured his son.

"What happened?" asked Alex.

Reggie explained that he had gotten a little dizzy and sick at work, but he was sure he just needed some rest. As Reggie headed back up the stairs, he stumbled and fell, clutching his chest.

"Dad, what's wrong?" cried Jamal, but his father grimaced and didn't answer.

"Grandma! Grandma, come quick!" Jamal called up the stairs in a panic.

Grandma CeCe ran to the top of the stairs. When she saw Reggie lying on the steps, she let out a little scream. "We've got to get him to the hospital right away!" she told the frightened boys.

• • •

"Yes, I'm sure his name was Millard Fillmore Smith," Catherine said into the phone. She was standing in the foyer of the Canellan house, trying to speak in a deeper voice with an Irish accent, like Mrs. O'Boyle's. "I remember because he was named after my favorite president . . ."

Frank tried hard to stifle a laugh.

"I'm positive he was a Ritter Brush man," Catherine continued. "But he sold me a feather duster yesterday and now it looks like a plucked chicken. . . . Oh, all right, good-bye!"

Catherine hung up the phone. The man she spoke to at the Ritter Brush Company had told her they didn't have an employee named Millard Fillmore Smith. Frank flopped down on the couch and began to gripe. "It was a dopey idea anyway. Why would a robber come to your house and tell you his real name?"

Catherine froze in her tracks. Why hadn't she thought of it before! "If this guy is a crook, and he's pretending to be a salesman to get into people's houses, he *would* make up a fake name!" she said. "That's why there's no one at the company with that name."

"If that's true, and we can prove he's the real thief, I'll be off the hook!" Frank said.

Catherine was adding the new information to

the casebook when Dr. Canellan strode into the house. He stared at Catherine and Frank.

"Why are you two covered with coal dust?" Dr. Canellan finally sputtered.

"We were trailing the coal man," Catherine volunteered. "We thought he was the one who robbed our house. So we jumped into the back of the coal wagon so we could spy on him."

"Have you two both lost your minds!" Dr. Canellan exploded. "Running around the streets playing detectives, jumping in and out of coal trucks! You could have been hurt!"

Catherine walked over to her father and took his hand. "But we're fine, and we think we know who stole the tea set."

"I don't want to hear anymore about it!" Dr. Canellan said. He glared at Frank. "I've just come from the Home for Wayward Boys. It's all set. They'll be taking you there tomorrow."

"But, Father, we think we know who stole—"

"Catherine, that's enough!" Dr. Canellan yelled. "Go to your room!"

Catherine burst into tears and ran up to her room.

"Dr. Canellan?"

"What is it, Frank?"

"I just wanted to say how sorry I am," Frank said quietly. "I didn't mean for Catherine to do anything dangerous."

"It's much too late for apologies, Frank," Dr. Canellan answered coldly.

Frank knew there was nothing he could do to change Dr. Canellan's mind. All he could think about as he walked to the basement was how afraid he was of going to the Home for Wayward Boys.

Grandma CeCe was trying to reassure Jamal as they returned from taking Reggie to the hospital. "There is nothing to worry about," she said, laying her hand gently on Jamal's head.

"Then how come you or Mom won't tell me what Dr. Hughes said?" asked Jamal. "I overheard him telling you all something about an X ray before you went into his office."

"Well, that was nothing for you to worry about, baby."

"I am not a baby anymore!" Jamal yelled. "I have a right to know what's wrong with my father!"

Grandma CeCe was surprised by Jamal's outburst. But she knew he was right. He wasn't a baby anymore, and she had to tell him the truth. "When Dr. Hughes looked at your father's X rays, there was some sort of shadow over his heart. A dark spot that shouldn't be there. So they decided to keep him in the hospital overnight and run some more tests in the morning."

"Is that all he said?" asked Jamal.

"Yes, that's all." Grandma CeCe took Jamal's hand. "You don't have to worry. Your father is going to be all right. There is nothing to worry about."

"If you're not worried, then how come you took Dad to the hospital?" Jamal asked.

"Because I'm his mother," Grandma CeCe replied. "And when you're a parent, you have to make sure everything is okay. Your mom does the same thing for you, right?"

"Yeah, I guess so," Jamal answered.

Grandma looked at him and smiled. "You *know* so," she said. She turned and went into the kitchen.

Jamal flopped down on the couch. He knew his grandmother was telling him the truth, but he couldn't stop worrying about his father.

Chapter 8

Catherine sat at her desk with tears rolling down her cheeks. She was writing to Ghostwriter to let him know what had happened:

Frank is being sent away in the morning.
We failed.

A weak and wobbly Ghostwriter struggled to answer her:

Don't give up now!

Catherine knew Ghostwriter was right. If they gave up now, Frank would never be saved, but she didn't know what to do. As she sat thinking, she heard voices from the hallway outside her door. She ran to the door and opened it a crack so that she could hear.

"You made the right decision, Dr. Canellan," Mrs. O'Boyle said. "Frank's a bad penny and he always will be."

"But I feel so bad about sending him away," Dr. Canellan said as they walked past Catherine's door.

Catherine shut the door quietly. She had to think of something before it was too late! She was determined to get back on the case, but she wondered how she could do that without Frank's help. As she stood near the door thinking, she noticed the window and remembered how Frank climbed up the side of the house to her room.

Catherine grabbed her casebook from the desk and stuffed it into the pocket of her dress. She went to the window, opened it, and looked down. It was a scary climb, but she had to do it. She couldn't give up now.

Meanwhile, Frank was packing his few belongings into a burlap sack when he heard tapping at the basement window. His mouth dropped open when he saw Catherine crouched there, grinning. Frank rushed over to the window and helped her climb down into the basement.

"Thanks for the help," Catherine said as she tried to catch her breath. "That was the only way to come in without being seen."

Frank smiled at Catherine. She was the pluckiest girl he'd ever met. "I'm glad you came to say good-bye," he said.

"Good-bye? We haven't even solved the case yet," Catherine insisted. "If we give up, you'll be sent away, and we'll never see each other again."

"That's the worst part about it," Frank said sadly. "I'm going to miss having a friend as good as you. But we can't find the Ritter Brush man over the telephone. We can't get out of the house. We can't do anything."

"What about Ghostwriter and his friends?" Catherine asked hopefully. "They can help us."

Frank sighed wearily. "They can't help. They live in the future."

"But that's why they *can* help!" Catherine said as the idea jumped into her head. "They can find out if this case was ever solved."

"Huh?" Frank said.

"Remember when we went to the library this morning? We looked at last week's newspapers to see about the crimes that had already happened, right?"

"Right," Frank answered, not sure of what she was leading up to.

"Well," Catherine continued, growing excited, "since Ghostwriter's friends live in the future, they can go to the library and look in newspapers from 1928. They can find out if this case was ever solved, and who did it! Then they could send us the name of the thief. They may even be able to tell us when and where he was captured!"

"Yeah!" Frank said. "Let's write a message telling them what we need them to do, then get Ghostwriter to carry it ahead to 1996. If this works, I'll be able to prove I'm innocent!" Frank sat down and opened the casebook. Catherine sat next to him, and they began to write to Ghostwriter's friends.

Dear Future Friends,
  Many houses around us have been robbed of valuable things made of silver. Our main suspect is pretending to be a Ritter Brush salesman. He says his name is Millard Fillmore Smith. We think he is using a fake name. Please read old issues of the *Brooklyn Eagle* printed in 1928. Find out if the case was solved, and if so, who's the crook.
  Please hurry!
                              Thank you,
                              Frank and Catherine

"That's great!" Catherine said as they finished, but when she looked at Frank he was frowning.

"I don't think this is going to work," he said, pointing to the casebook. "Look at Ghostwriter."

Catherine turned back to the table and saw Ghostwriter's faint glow on the casebook. He kept trying to lift the words and spin back into the time tunnel, but every attempt failed. The message was too long for him to carry all the way to 1996.

"Maybe he'll be able to carry the message if we make it shorter," Frank suggested. "Let's cut out everything but the most important parts: the crime, the suspect, and what we want Ghostwriter's friends to do."

Catherine agreed with Frank, and they set about trying to make the message as short as possible.

Crime:
houses robbed
silver
Suspect:
Ritter Brush man
Millard Fillmore Smith
IMPOSTOR?
Job:
Read <u>Brooklyn Eagle</u>, 1928.
Was case solved?
Who did it?
HURRY!

"Well, that's everything important," Catherine said when they finished editing the message. "But is it short enough for Ghostwriter to carry?"

They watched anxiously as Ghostwriter swirled around the words, trying to pick them up. It was a struggle, but finally Ghostwriter began spinning faster and faster. Suddenly, in a flash of light, he was gone.

"Hotchacha!" Frank shouted as he and Catherine jumped for joy.

They sat on the bed looking at the casebook, waiting for Ghostwriter. Frank grew sad as he thought about his situation. "I hope Ghostwriter's friends can help us," he said to Catherine. "I don't have much time."

Catherine looked at Frank. "Promise me you won't run away, no matter what happens."

"Don't worry about me," Frank said.

"Promise?" Catherine pleaded.

"I promise," Frank said as he put his hand behind his back and crossed his fingers.

Catherine smiled and headed for the window above the staircase. "Thanks. I'd better get back upstairs before someone discovers I'm missing."

Frank helped Catherine climb up on the banister and out the basement window. He watched as she waved and ran out of the alley. "Bye, Catherine," he said sadly.

• • •

Lenni, Gaby, Alex, and Tina were sitting around the kitchen table in Lenni's loft when Ghostwriter returned in a flash of light. "Ghostwriter's back!" Alex cried.

"He looks sick," Gaby said. Ghostwriter floated around the room, barely visible, a glimmer of his former self. He slowly melted into Lenni's computer and began typing.

"This must be a message from Frank and Catherine," Alex said as they gathered around the screen.

"I'll copy it into the casebook," Tina volunteered.

As Ghostwriter revealed Catherine and Frank's message, the team started shouting out questions: "What's a Ritter Brush man? What's a *Brooklyn Eagle*?"

"I think we'd better get to the library and find out the information Frank and Catherine need," Lenni said.

"And we'd better quick," Tina added.

Lenni, Gaby, Tina, and Alex charged into the Carroll Street Library and up to the librarian's desk.

"Excuse me. Can you tell us what a Ritter Brush man is?" Tina inquired.

"Yes," the librarian answered. "He's a salesman

who went door-to-door selling household items like brushes, mops, things like that."

"Have you ever heard of a book or a magazine called the—" Alex paused as he checked the casebook to make sure he had the right name, "*Brooklyn Eagle*? We've never heard of it."

"The *Brooklyn Eagle* was a very popular newspaper, but they stopped printing it around 1955," the librarian said. "The library keeps copies of the *Brooklyn Eagle* in ledgers. They're very old and fragile. But, if you promise to handle them very carefully . . ."

"We promise," Alex said eagerly. "Do you have copies from 1928?"

"Why don't you have a seat, and I'll see what I can find," the librarian said, and headed into the back room where the periodicals were stored.

When the librarian returned, she was carrying two huge, dusty ledgers. Alex and Gaby started looking through one of the ledgers, while Lenni and Tina searched through the other.

The work was slow going, because everyone kept getting distracted by interesting articles about important events in 1928. Finally Alex came up with an idea. "Let's only look for the headlines about crimes," he suggested. "Headlines tell what the story is about in a few words."

"Right," Tina agreed. "Look for headlines

with words like *burglaries, silver,* and *impostors*."

The kids searched through the fragile old newspapers reading headline after headline: MASKED ROBBER REVEALED! HILLSIDE GANG CAPTURED, COPS CAPTURE CANE AFTER GUN-FIGHT, KIDNAPPERS GET LIFE, CORNWELL DIA-MOND STOLEN.

"I think I found it!" Lenni whispered excitedly. Alex, Tina, and Gaby crowded around her to get a good look at the article.

YOUNGSTERS HELP
CAPTURE RITTER
BRUSH IMPOSTOR

Raynard Wilcox, who pretended to be a Ritter Brush man named Millard Fillmore Smith, was captured July 12 at the Silver Imports Warehouse. He was charged with stealing from several homes in Brooklyn. The police were aided by a tip from two neighborhood children, Catherine Canellan and Frank Flynn. When asked how they were able to crack the case, the youngsters mysteriously replied that they couldn't have done it without the help of some friends who are far ahead of their time.

"Hey, they were talking about us! We're the ones who are 'far ahead of their time,'" Tina said. She began copying all of the information into the casebook.

"That's so cool!" Lenni said. "We're in the newspaper more than fifty years before we were born!"

"Hey, something strange is happening," Tina said, pointing to the newspaper article. "I just finished writing down Catherine's and Frank's names, and now they've disappeared!"

Sure enough, Frank's and Catherine's names had disappeared from the article, along with other words. "The headline is gone, too!" Lenni pointed out.

"How can that happen?" Alex wondered aloud.

"Is Ghostwriter taking the words away?" Gaby asked.

"No, Ghostwriter is resting at my place," Lenni said.

"Maybe the past is changing because we haven't sent Catherine and Frank this information yet," Tina guessed.

"Huh?" said Gaby, who had never heard of anything so ridiculous.

"I get it," said Lenni. "If we don't send this information to Frank and Catherine soon, it will be too late. This article will never exist."

"And that impostor, Raynard Wilcox, won't be captured," added Alex.

"How come I'm the only one that doesn't get it?" Gaby frowned.

"We'll explain it later," Tina said. As she looked

down at the article, it continued to disappear word by word. "But right now, we'd better hurry and get this information to Ghostwriter."

"Why don't we just send it to him from here?" Alex asked.

"Because he's resting," Lenni said. "Come on, we've got the legs, so let's use them!"

Tina, Alex, and Gaby hurriedly gathered their belongings and followed Lenni back to the loft.

Over at Jamal's house, Grandma CeCe was frowning as she hung up the phone. "Jamal!" she called as she sat down on the couch and started putting on her shoes.

Jamal ran into the living room. "What's wrong? Where are you going?" he asked.

"To the hospital," Grandma replied. "I just got off the phone with your mother. She said your father is unconscious. They can't wake him up."

"Because of his heart?" Jamal asked, his voice shaking.

"I'm not sure," Grandma CeCe said as she grabbed her purse and car keys.

"Can I go with you?" Jamal asked.

"No, Jamal."

"Look, Grandma, I want to be with Dad," he insisted. "Besides, you're gonna be there, and Mom's already there."

Grandma CeCe looked at Jamal, and her face softened. "All right," she said. "Let's hurry."

Lenni, Alex, Gaby, and Tina rushed back to Lenni's loft and headed straight for the computer. Tina opened the casebook to the notes she had taken at the library. She set the book down next to the screen and said, "Okay, Ghostwriter, it's up to you."

The team watched nervously as a very weak Ghostwriter read Tina's notes:

The Ritter Brush man's real name is Raynard Wilcox. He was captured at the Silver Imports Warehouse July 12. Tell Catherine and Frank to tell the police right away!

As soon as he finished reading the message, Ghostwriter started spinning around the letters. He kept trying to lift the words so he could carry them back to 1928, but the words kept falling back onto the page.

"He can't do it," Gaby cried. "He's too weak."

"But if he doesn't get this information back to 1928, Frank and Catherine won't be able to solve the case," Tina said.

"I don't care about the case," Gaby protested. "I care about Ghostwriter. He just can't do it!"

"But he has to do it. Ghostwriter said helping

Frank and Catherine would save the team," Tina reminded Gaby.

Ghostwriter flew back into the computer and began typing a message:

```
help
  Fra k become
     doc
        tor.
Must
```

The team watched Ghostwriter's scattered message appear.

"I think he's trying to say,'Must help Frank become a doctor,'" Lenni said. "He wants us to keep trying. Maybe making the message shorter will help." Lenni sat down at the keyboard and began to type a shorter version of the message using just the important facts.

"What does Frank's becoming a doctor have to do with the team?" Alex asked as Lenni typed.

"Frank's last name is Flynn," Tina said to Alex. "I don't go to a Dr. Flynn. Do you?"

"No," answered Alex.

"Never heard of him," Lenni said as she finished typing. "I've made this message as short as I can. I hope Ghostwriter can carry it now." They all watched as Ghostwriter's glow surrounded the shorter message:

Raynard Wilcox
Silver Imports Warehouse
July 12

Ghostwriter began to spin around the words faster and faster. Finally the swirl of dancing letters disappeared in a flash of light.

"Yes!" Lenni shouted triumphantly. "I hope he makes it all the way there."

"I hope he makes it all the way back," Gaby said, worried that she would never see Ghostwriter again.

Chapter 9

"Ghostwriter!"** Catherine shouted as the whirling ball of light flew into her bedroom and landed on the casebook. She ran to the writing table and watched as Ghostwriter weakly scrawled the message across the page.

> Raynard Wilcox
> Silver Imports Warehouse,
> July 12

"July 12!" Catherine cried as she read the message. "That's tomorrow!" Catherine quickly copied the message into the casebook. When she finished, she grabbed the book and ran out of her room.

In the basement, Lucy crept over to Frank's hiding place in the wall and removed the brick. She took the letter she hadn't returned earlier out of her pocket and shoved it into the space in the wall.

"Frank! Frank!" Lucy heard Catherine's voice calling from upstairs. Lucy quickly picked up the brick and ran to hide by the coal chute just as Catherine dashed into the basement. "Frank!" she shouted. "Ghostwriter came back! Ghostwriter came back! Frank!"

"Who's Ghostwriter?" Lucy asked as she came out of her hiding place.

"What are you doing here?" Catherine demanded, her eyes flashing with anger. "Where's Frank?"

"All of his things are gone," Lucy said with a little smile. "I think he ran away."

Catherine gasped and ran to the open basement window. "Frank! Frank come back!" she called out into the night air. "I've got the information that will prove you're innocent! Frank, we can solve the case now. Frank!"

"You'd better stop yelling," Lucy warned. "You don't want Father and Mrs. O'Boyle to hear you."

"But I have to find Frank," Catherine cried desperately. "I've got information that will prove he's innocent."

"It's too late for that now. He's gone for good," Lucy said. She went over to the wall where Frank's letters had been hidden and pushed the brick back into the wall.

"What are you doing?" Catherine asked.

"Closing up Frank's secret hiding place," Lucy said, savoring the fact that she finally knew something about Frank that Catherine didn't know. "He kept his diary and all his mother's letters in there. I read them all, whenever he wasn't around."

"Those things were private!" Catherine scolded. "How could you do something so rotten?"

"Well, you two are always whispering and keeping secrets from me!" Lucy argued. "That's pretty rotten, too. You're just mad because I found out things about Frank that you don't even know."

"What kind of things?" Catherine asked.

"I can't tell you. They're private," Lucy taunted. She headed for the stairs.

Catherine rushed after her. "Look, Lucy, let's not fight right now. Maybe something you read could help me find Frank."

"Maybe," Lucy said.

"Lucy, you've got to help," Catherine pleaded. "I can prove Frank's innocent, so he won't have to go to the Home for Wayward Boys."

"I want him to go," Lucy spat.

"Why?"

"Because you like him better than me and you never play with me anymore," Lucy said.

Catherine stared at Lucy. "I'm sorry, Lucy," she said slowly. "I didn't mean to leave you out. But I promise, if you help me find Frank, I'll play with you and never keep secrets from you ever again. Cross my heart and hope to die."

Lucy eyed her sister suspiciously for a moment, not sure if she could trust her. "If you really mean what you say, then tell me who Ghostwriter is."

Catherine hesitated. Ghostwriter was supposed to be a secret, but she had no choice. "All right." Catherine sighed. "I'll tell you as much as I can. But you've got to promise you won't tell anybody."

"I promise," Lucy said as she followed Catherine to Frank's writing table. "Is he a good ghost or a bad ghost?"

"A good ghost," Catherine replied as she sat down and opened the casebook. "And he and his friends are trying to help us prove Frank is innocent."

"A ghost with friends?" Lucy asked.

"Yes," Catherine insisted. "His friends all live in the future, in 1996."

"You're making this up so I'll help you," Lucy said.

"No, I'm not. It's true," Catherine said urgently. "He sends us messages from the future.

And the only way to communicate with him is through writing. But you can't see him. He's invisible to everybody except Frank and me."

"Let me write to him and see for myself," Lucy demanded. She reached for the casebook and wrote:

> **Ghostwriter, my name is Lucy. If you're real, let me see you.**

"Well, where is he?" Lucy taunted as she waited for something to happen.

"I told you," Catherine said. "You can't see him. I wouldn't lie to you."

"Yes you would," Lucy shouted as she pushed the chair back and headed for the staircase. "You're a big phony!"

Catherine ran after Lucy and grabbed her shoulder. "Lucy, please. I'm begging you."

Lucy turned to brush Catherine's hand off. Her eyes widened and she gasped. The letters on the casebook were glowing and floating up into the air. The words were wobbly, but Ghostwriter used all the strength he had left to send a message that would convince Lucy he was real:

> Lucy, please help.

Lucy stared at the floating words, her mouth open. "He *is* real!" she cried.

"Now will you help me?" Catherine asked.

"Yes," Lucy replied. She watched as Ghost-writer's message floated back down into the case-book and disappeared. "I'll do anything you want."

Lucy rushed back to the secret hiding place, pulled the brick out of the wall, reached inside, and took out a letter. "This is the only letter I have. I dropped it when I was putting it back in the secret hiding place this morning. I don't think it's going to help."

Catherine sat at the writing table and opened the casebook. "Read it out loud. There might be a clue in there that will help us find Frank."

Lucy took the letter out of the envelope and read it out loud.

Dear Elizabeth,

I hope you and Frank are well. It's been such a long time since I laid eyes on you. I try to have a new letter ready to mail to you every time we pull into a station.

The conductor says there's lots of work for fellows like me in California. As soon as I arrive, I'm going to find a job and save every penny. Then I'll come back for you and Frank and we'll enjoy the Twentieth Century together.

Love,
Sean Flynn

"So Frank's father was on his way to California to try to find work," Catherine said.

"And he was on a train," Lucy added, "because he said he was mailing the letters from a 'station' and he mentioned a 'conductor.'"

"Good!" Catherine said as she noted the facts in the casebook. "And he was going to save all his money so he could come back for them and they could enjoy the rest of their lives together."

Lucy took another look at the letter. "It doesn't say 'enjoy the rest of our lives together,'" Lucy pointed out. "It says 'enjoy the Twentieth Century together.'"

"Well, we're living in the twentieth century," Catherine countered. "So he means he wants the family to enjoy the rest of their lives together."

"But look at the way he wrote it," Lucy persisted. "The words *Twentieth Century* are capitalized as if they were a name. Like the one on the poster by Frank's bed."

Catherine went to take a closer look at the poster with the picture of the speeding train. "Lucy, you're right!" she exclaimed. "That must be the name of the train Frank's father was on. And Frank could be on that train heading for California to try to find his father."

"The railroad station is only a few blocks from here," Lucy said. "If we hurry, we might be able to catch him."

"Frank! Frank!" Dr. Canellan called from the top of the stairs. Catherine and Lucy grimaced.

"Uh-oh," Catherine whispered. "If Father finds out Frank ran away, he won't let us go after him."

"I have a plan," Lucy said. She hurried over to Frank's bed and pulled back the covers. "You keep Father upstairs." Lucy quickly climbed into Frank's bed and pulled the covers over her head. Catherine rushed up the stairs and met her father just as he opened the basement door.

"What are you doing down here?" Dr. Canellan asked, a little annoyed.

"I uh . . . ," Catherine started as she tried to come up with an excuse. "I um . . . I came down to talk to Frank."

Dr. Canellan looked down into the basement and noticed the body under the covers. "We'd better let him sleep," Dr. Canellan whispered. "We can come back later."

Catherine sighed with relief as she followed her father out of the basement. As soon as the door slammed, Lucy peered from under the covers, then leaped out of the bed. She rushed to the writing table and grabbed the casebook. She ran to the basement window, opened it, and climbed out as fast as she could.

• • •

Jamal was pale and scared when he and Grandma CeCe returned from the hospital. "Dad looked really sick, Grandma," he said.

"I know, but there's nothing we can do about it tonight," Grandma CeCe said wearily as she put down her purse. "In the morning they'll take more tests and X rays. I'm sure they won't find anything serious."

"But what if they do?" Jamal asked.

Grandma CeCe sat heavily in an armchair and looked at Jamal. "The doctors will do everything they can to get him well. And you know with your mom working at the hospital he's going to get the best care there is."

"Grandma," Jamal said as he sat on the edge of the coffee table and took one of Grandma CeCe's hands, "I want you to promise to tell me the truth about everything. No matter how bad it might be. I'm old enough. I can take it."

"I promise," Grandma CeCe replied. "And you know, Jamal, I'm proud of the way you've handled things. I'm going to have to start treating you like the mature young man that you are."

"Thanks, Grandma," Jamal said. He squeezed his grandmother's hand, and they sat quietly, thinking about his father.

• • •

Dr. Canellan paced in front of the sofa as he listened to Catherine's story. "And Raynard Wilcox pretended to be a Ritter Brush man?" he asked, unconvinced.

"Yes, that's how he got into other people's houses," Catherine said. "And when they left the room, he would steal any valuable silver that they had on hand."

"That's a pretty far-fetched tale, Catherine."

"But Father," Catherine cried, "you've got to believe me and call the police."

"Where did you get all this information?" Dr. Canellan asked.

"I was reading about neighborhood burglaries in the *Police Gazette* and then . . ." Catherine stopped talking when she realized what she had just admitted.

"The *Police Gazette*?" Dr. Canellan asked sternly. "You read that?"

"Well, I was in the library, but . . ." Catherine saw the doubt in her father's eyes, and she knew it was time to come clean. "Remember the *Police Gazette* that Lucy found in the basement?" Dr. Canellan nodded. "That was mine, not Frank's. I've been reading them since long before he came to live with us."

"Oh, Catherine," Dr. Canellan said, his voice full of disappointment.

"I'm sorry, Father," Catherine said. "I'm crazy

for crime stories and mysteries. But we can't talk about this right now. Come on, you've got to call the police!"

Dr. Canellan looked at Catherine. Her eyes flashed with determination. "All right, all right," he said, and headed for the phone. "I'll call the police. Run downstairs and get Frank. He should be here when the police arrive."

Catherine was sure Frank couldn't be back yet. She stood in the middle of the living room and called him, pretending he was in the basement. "Frank! Frank!" she shouted.

"Don't shout, for goodness' sake," Dr. Canellan scolded as he dialed the phone. "Go and get him."

Catherine took a timid step toward the foyer and called weakly, "Frank."

"Quit your bellyaching," Frank said as he burst in from the basement. "I'm here!"

"Frank, you're back!" Catherine shouted with glee. They ran to each other, grabbed hands, and jumped up and down.

"Children, please," Dr. Canellan called.

"Lucy found me at the railroad station," Frank whispered. "I thought she was up to one of her dirty tricks again, until she showed me the casebook and told me Ghostwriter wanted her to help us."

"I'm so glad you came back," Catherine said. "Ghostwriter and his friends sent us the information we needed. Father's on the phone telling the police. I hope they'll help us."

"If they don't, I'm really sunk this time," Frank said. He and Catherine watched Dr. Canellan and held their breath.

Chapter 10

"I'll get it," Jamal shouted as he bounded down the stairs toward the front door. When he opened the door, he was surprised to find Lenni, Alex, Gaby, and Tina on the stoop. "Hi, guys," he said with a bright smile. "I thought you were my dad."

"Is he coming home?" Alex asked.

"Yep! My mom called and said that he just got better all of a sudden," Jamal explained. "They took another X ray this morning, and the shadow on his heart had disappeared. Just like it was never there in the first place."

"What a relief," Tina said.

"That's great, Jamal," Alex chimed in.

"Thanks," Jamal said as he led his friends into the living room. "What about Ghostwriter?" he asked.

"We haven't heard from him," Gaby said sadly.

"It was real hard for him to take a message back to 1928," Lenni said. "We're not even sure if he made it back to Frank and Catherine."

"Speaking of Frank, that reminds me," Alex said, turning to Jamal. "Have you ever heard of a Dr. Flynn?"

"No," Jamal replied.

"Dr. Frank Flynn?" Grandma CeCe asked. Jamal and his friends were surprised to find her at the living room door, listening.

"Yeah, that's him," Alex said. "How do you know his name?"

"Oh, I will never forget him," Grandma CeCe said as she stepped into the room. "He saved Jamal's father's life a long, long time ago."

"What?" Jamal asked, shocked.

Grandma CeCe sat down and began to explain. "When your father was born, he had a tiny hole in his heart. By the time he was four years old, he was so sick we were afraid we were going to lose him. And no doctor would operate on him because he was so little. Your grandfather and I worried ourselves so. We thought our son was going to die. Then we met Dr.

Frank Flynn. He was the head of surgery at the Brooklyn Children's Hospital, and he'd been experimenting with new surgery techniques. He persuaded us to let him operate, and everything worked out fine. If it weren't for Dr. Flynn, Reggie wouldn't be alive today. Why were you kids asking about him?"

"Ah . . . ," Tina stalled.

"Well, um . . . see . . . uh," Lenni tried.

"Well, never mind," Grandma CeCe said, giving the team a puzzled look. "I've got to start preparing for Reggie's welcome-home celebration. Why don't you kids stick around and help decorate the house."

"We'll be glad to help," Tina volunteered.

"Great," Grandma CeCe said as she went into the kitchen. "I'm going to bake the biggest cake you have ever seen!"

When Grandma CeCe was gone, the team members stared at each other, dumbfounded. "Man, this is too weird," Jamal said.

"Yeah," Alex agreed. "But now we know what Ghostwriter meant when he said helping Frank would save the team. If Frank hadn't become a doctor, your father would have died when he was four years old. *You* wouldn't have been born!"

"And *we* wouldn't have met Ghostwriter," Lenni added, "which means no team."

"Right," Tina agreed.

"What about Ghostwriter?" Lenni stood up and

turned to the team. "He saved the team, and now we have to rescue him!"

"How do we start?" Tina asked.

"I got it!" Gaby shouted. "Grandma CeCe said Dr. Flynn worked at the Brooklyn Children's Hospital. If we go there and find him, he might be able to tell us what happened to Ghostwriter. And maybe he can help us get him back."

"Great idea, Gaby," Alex said as he leaped up from the couch. "Let's go see if we can track him down."

Gaby and Alex headed for the door. Gaby turned back to the team with a big smile. "If we're lucky, we might bring Ghostwriter *and* Frank back to the party with us!" Jamal, Lenni, and Tina wished them luck.

An hour later, a "Welcome Home Reggie" sign was draped across the entrance to the living room and balloons and streamers hung from the ceiling. Jamal, Lenni, Tina, and Grandma CeCe gathered around Reggie, who was sitting on the couch.

"Dad, you look great!" Jamal said as he hugged his father.

"And I feel great!" Reggie exclaimed, beaming. "I'm telling you, all of a sudden I got better. As if

I had never been sick in the first place. I hope you didn't worry too much."

"Oh, I wasn't worried at all," Grandma CeCe teased. "I knew everything would work out fine."

Reggie looked at his mother and laughed. "You *know* you were worried about me. You probably started writing my obituary."

Everyone laughed, except Tina, who had never heard of an obituary. Reggie explained, "That's a notice people place in the newspaper when somebody dies. It tells about the person's life and the family members they left behind."

"Oh," Tina said. "I've seen those before, but I didn't know what they were called."

"Don't you think you should go upstairs and lie down?" Grandma CeCe asked Reggie.

"No, I'm telling you, I feel great!" Reggie replied. "And I am hungry enough to eat that whole cake you're baking."

"Who told you I was baking a cake?" Grandma CeCe asked innocently.

"My nose told me." Reggie chuckled as he got up and followed the scent to the kitchen door. "Yep, there is a caramel cake in that kitchen with my name on it."

"Now you wait a minute," Grandma CeCe said as she chased Reggie into the kitchen. "We can't cut the cake until Doris gets home!"

The doorbell rang, and Jamal jumped up and

ran for the door. It was Alex and Gaby. "Hey, my dad's back and he's feeling great!" Jamal announced.

"I'm glad to hear it," Gaby said.

"Did you find Frank?" Lenni asked.

Gaby and Alex looked at each other sadly. They walked into the living room and sat down.

"What's the matter?" Tina asked.

"Frank died on May first of last year," Alex answered quietly.

"But . . . ," Lenni said, "it's like we just wrote to him. It seemed as if he was a kid like us."

"In 1928 he *was* a kid like us," Alex responded.

"Man, I really wanted to meet him," Jamal moaned. "To thank him."

The team sat silently, thinking about their friend from the past. They couldn't get over the fact that he had died. Suddenly Lenni jumped up. "Ghostwriter!" she shouted. "How are we going to find Ghostwriter now?"

"Well, maybe Frank got married and told his family about Ghostwriter," Jamal suggested. "If we get in touch with them, they might help us find him."

"How can we find out about his family?" Alex asked.

"We can read his obituary in the newspaper!" Tina yelled. "Jamal's dad just told us that family members are mentioned in the obituaries. Let's get to the library and see if we can find a copy of his obituary in a newspaper."

Everyone headed for the library, except Jamal, who wanted to spend some more time with his dad. Before Lenni, Tina, Gaby, and Alex left, they made him promise to save them some of Grandma CeCe's caramel cake.

Chapter 11

"**H**ere it is," the librarian said as she approached the table where Lenni, Gaby, Tina, and Alex waited anxiously. "A copy of Dr. Frank Flynn's obituary from *The New York Times*."

The team thanked her as they gathered together to read the obituary.

FRANK FLYNN, 76,
HEART SURGERY PIONEER

Dr. Frank Flynn, former head of surgery at Brooklyn Children's Hospital, died of natural causes on Sunday at a hospital in Brooklyn. He was 76 years old.

> Born in Cork, Ireland, and raised in Brooklyn, New York, Dr. Flynn dedicated his career to helping those who could not afford medical care and was one of the pioneers of heart surgery for children. He is survived by his wife, Catherine Canellan Flynn, an author.

"Frank and Catherine got married?" Tina asked, surprised.

"Looks that way," Alex said.

"Catherine would definitely know about Ghostwriter and what happened to him," Gaby said.

"The obituary said she's an author," Lenni stated. "Maybe the librarian can tell us how to find her."

The team agreed that it was worth a shot. They went to the librarian's desk and asked her how to go about finding an author.

"By contacting the publisher," the librarian replied. "They'll send a letter on to the author. You can find the publisher by looking in the front of a book written by the author you're looking for."

"Great!" said Alex. "Do you have any books written by Catherine Canellan Flynn?"

"Of course we do," the librarian answered. "She writes wonderful detective stories. As a matter of fact, she does most of her research right here in this library." The librarian stood and looked around the room. "Do you see that lady at the table over there?" she pointed across the room, where an elegant gray-haired woman was sitting at a table surrounded by books. She was wearing reading eyeglasses and taking notes. "That's Catherine Canellan Flynn," said the librarian.

"Are you serious?" Lenni asked.

"Yes, that's her," the librarian said.

The team started jumping up and down cheering. "This is a *library*! It's supposed to be *quiet,*" the librarian whispered, trying not to laugh. The team quieted down as they approached Catherine Canellan Flynn.

"Excuse me," Gaby said nervously.

Catherine peered at Gaby over her glasses and smiled. "Yes?" she asked.

"We're the Ghostwriter Team," Gaby said. Catherine's smile faded as she looked around at the kids' earnest faces.

"We helped you prove Frank didn't steal the tea set," Alex reminded her. Catherine was stunned. She sat back in her seat and removed her glasses.

"Don't you remember?" Gaby pleaded.

"I remember Ghostwriter," Catherine said, slowly rubbing her eyes as if she couldn't quite believe what she was hearing. "And I remember he had friends who sent messages . . . oh, but that couldn't have been you."

"Yes, it was us!" cried Tina. "We sent you the message about the impostor!"

"You?" Catherine asked, astounded. The team nodded.

"Well, *hotchacha!*" Catherine exclaimed as she stood and hugged the team members. "You *are* Ghostwriter's friends! How did you find me?"

"We read Frank's obituary in the newspaper and found out you two got married," Lenni said. "We're sorry he died."

"We felt like he was one of us," Alex said.

"Yeah," Tina added. "He was a great doctor."

Catherine smiled at the memory of her husband. "Frank and I had a wonderful life together, because of you and Ghostwriter."

"We need to know what happened to Ghostwriter after he sent the message about Raynard Wilcox," Alex said.

Catherine shivered. "Raynard Wilcox. Do you know that man's name still sends shivers down my spine? He almost got away." Catherine and the team sat down, and Catherine told them this story about what happened on July 12, 1928:

Frank and Catherine had convinced Dr. Canellan to take them to the big, dark warehouse where Raynard Wilcox was hiding out. The three of them hid across the street and watched the two policemen who were in charge of the search. One of the policemen went into the warehouse, and the other one went around the back to make sure Wilcox wouldn't escape.

"I must have been out of my mind to let you two talk me into bringing you here," Dr. Canellan complained.

"What do you mean?" Catherine asked. "We solved the case. We deserve to see the dirty bum get captured."

"There's no guarantee he's in there," Dr. Canellan warned. "He may never be caught."

"Oh, he's in there all right," Frank snarled. "And I can hardly wait to see the mug get put in handcuffs."

"Settle down, Frank," Dr. Canellan said.

Suddenly a shrill police whistle blew. Across the street the door of the warehouse burst open, and a heavyset man carrying a Ritter Brush suitcase ran into the street.

"That must be Raynard Wilcox!" Frank cried.

A dazed policeman staggered out of the building, blowing his whistle and rubbing his head where Wilcox had hit it. The other policeman ran into the street and chased Raynard Wilcox. When Wilcox saw that the policeman was gaining on him, he stopped abruptly, turned, and shoved his suitcase into the policeman, pushing him to the ground.

"He's getting away!" Catherine shouted. Frank jumped up and took off after him.

"Frank, come back!" Dr. Canellan yelled as he and Catherine ran after him.

Frank's legs churned and he gasped for breath as he chased Wilcox. If he got away, Frank would never be able to prove that he hadn't stolen the tea set.

Wilcox darted a glance back and saw Frank gaining on him. He sneered and started to speed up, but Frank was faster, and with a flying tackle he jumped on Wilcox's back and pushed him down to the ground. The Ritter Brush suitcase flew out of Wilcox's hand and landed on the ground with a crash. Silver candlesticks, silver serving trays, and a silver tea set spilled onto the ground.

The two policemen grabbed Wilcox and slapped a pair of handcuffs onto his wrists. Catherine and Dr. Canellan helped Frank up off the ground.

"Are you all right?" Catherine asked.

"Sure, I'm swell," Frank said as he brushed off his clothes.

"You're a hero, my boy!" Dr. Canellan said proudly as he clapped Frank on the shoulder.

As the policemen led Raynard Wilcox away in handcuffs, Wilcox struggled toward Frank. "You had no business butting in," he growled threateningly. "I'll get you for this, kid!"

"Aw, save the gas!" Frank hollered.

"Yeah, shut your face, you big windbag!" Dr. Canellan shouted. Catherine and Frank looked at the doctor in shock. Dr. Canellan looked at Frank and Catherine and laughed. *"Hotchacha!"* he shouted, and he punched his fist into the air.

"I guess I'm a bad influence on you, too, huh, Doc?" Frank cracked. Dr. Canellan smiled down at Frank and Catherine. He put his arms around both of them, and they headed for home.

Lucy was reading in the living room when they arrived.

"Mrs. O'Boyle! Lucy!" Catherine shouted jubilantly. "We did it!"

"Did you catch the thief?" Lucy asked.

"Frank caught him," Dr. Canellan said happily.

"He tackled him right before he got away!" Catherine said, looking at Frank with pride.

Lucy looked at Frank, who was blushing. She walked over to him and held out her hand. "I'm sorry for all the bad things I did to you," she said.

"I'm sorry for all the bad things you did to me, too," Frank said coldly. After a moment he smiled and shook Lucy's hand. "But I forgive you, I guess."

"Thanks, I guess," Lucy said, smiling at Frank.

"What's all the commotion?" Mrs. O'Boyle asked as she came in from the kitchen.

"We're celebrating," Dr. Canellan declared. "Frank is not going to the Home for Wayward Boys. He's staying right here with this family, where he belongs."

"Hotchacha!" Frank and Catherine cheered at the same time.

"Frank, I owe you an apology," Dr. Canellan said as he walked toward the boy. "You're a good and honest boy. And if we ever have any more problems, we'll solve them together, like a family."

"Thanks, Doc," Frank said as he shook hands with Dr. Canellan.

Mrs. O'Boyle shook her head sourly and headed out of the room. "You're not going away are you?" Lucy wailed.

"I'm not going anywhere," Mrs. O'Boyle proclaimed. "Someone's got to make sure that Frank stays on the straight and narrow. And clean his filthy coal-dust footprints off the floor!"

"That wasn't my footprint!" Frank protested.

"Now, Frank, don't start lying," Mrs. O'Boyle argued.

"He's telling the truth," Dr. Canellan said. "The footprint was mine."

"Yours?" Catherine said, surprised.

"I'm afraid so," the doctor confessed. "I went into the coal cellar with my shoes on. I'm the one who broke the rules."

"Well!" huffed Mrs. O'Boyle. "I'll have to keep

the both of you on the straight and narrow now, won't I?" She turned abruptly and headed up the stairs, with Lucy following at her heels.

Catherine, Frank, and Dr. Canellan burst out laughing. "Come on, let's go get some lemonade!" Dr. Canellan shouted.

"Hotchacha!" Frank exclaimed, and they all dashed into the kitchen.

Chapter 12

"**T**hat was the beginning of the best times of my life." Catherine sighed as she finished telling the team how Raynard Wilcox was captured.

"I'm glad everything worked out," Lenni said. "If Frank hadn't grown up to become a doctor, our friend's father might not be alive today."

"I don't understand," Catherine said.

"Frank was the doctor who operated on his heart and saved him when he was a little boy," Lenni said.

"If our friend Jamal's father had died, we probably wouldn't have ever met Ghostwriter," concluded Alex.

"But what about Ghostwriter?" Gaby asked.

"Yes, where is he?" Catherine wondered wistfully. "Oh, I would love to see him again."

"We don't know where he is," Tina said.

"He never came back after we sent you the last message," Gaby added. "That's why we were trying to find you—to see if you knew what happened to him."

"I don't know," Catherine said with concern. "Frank and I went on writing to him, but he never answered. And so, we assumed that, well, he'd gone back to 1996." Catherine sat for a moment looking at Lenni, Alex, Tina, and Gaby. Then she had a brainstorm. "Oh my gosh! Oh, this *is* 1996! And here we are all in the same room for real this time!"

"Except for Ghostwriter," Lenni reminded them.

Catherine smiled as she thought back to her youth. "I will never forget the first time Ghostwriter popped out of Frank's diary. I was so frightened."

"I wish we had Frank's diary now," Gaby said sadly. "Because if that's how Ghostwriter first got to 1928, maybe that's how he tried to come back, and he got stuck or something."

"Gaby could be right!" Lenni said as she turned to Catherine. "Do you have Frank's diary at home?"

"Oh, I haven't seen that diary since I was your age," Catherine replied. "But it's probably still in Frank's secret hiding place. It was behind a loose brick in the wall of the basement. The wall opposite the staircase, if I remember correctly."

Lenni, Gaby, Alex, and Tina looked at each other with excitement. "Will you show us where the hiding place is?" Gaby asked.

"I don't live in that house anymore," Catherine said.

"That's no problem," Tina said. "Our friend Jamal lives there now."

"You've just got to help us save Ghostwriter!" Gaby pleaded.

"Well, there isn't anything I wouldn't do for Ghostwriter," Catherine said as she gathered her books and put her reading glasses away. "Let's skedaddle!" They all rushed out of the library together.

At the Jenkinses' house, Catherine watched carefully as Jamal, Lenni, Tina, Alex, and Gaby ran their hands along the brick walls of the basement.

"Are you sure it's in this wall?" Jamal asked as he climbed on top of the washer and dryer that stood in the exact same place as had Frank's bed in 1928.

"Yes, I'm sure," said Catherine. "Just keep looking for a loose brick, farther down."

"I found it!" Gaby shouted as a brick wobbled beneath her hand. The team crowded around and watched as she pulled the brick out of the wall. Gaby reached into the hole and pulled out a yellowed newspaper clipping. "It's the *Brooklyn Eagle* article about Raynard Wilcox's capture!" Gaby said. She passed the article to Catherine.

"Oh, Frank and I were so proud." Catherine sighed. "We must've bought a hundred copies of this paper."

"All the words are back!" Alex said, looking at the article over Catherine's shoulder.

"That's because everything worked out the way it should," Tina said.

"Almost everything . . . ," Gaby said. She reached back into the secret hiding place. This time she pulled out an old dust-covered book. Gaby turned to Catherine and held it out for her to see. "Is this the diary?"

"Yes," Catherine answered. "That's Frank's diary."

"Well, what are we waiting for?" Alex asked impatiently. "Let's open it."

"I'm scared," Gaby said. "If this doesn't help us find Ghostwriter, then he's gone forever."

Catherine put a hand on Gaby's shoulder and looked her in the eye. "The sooner we look inside, the sooner we're going to know, kiddo."

Gaby took a deep breath and placed the diary on a shelf. Catherine stepped forward, and she and

Gaby gently blew the dust off the cover. Then, very carefully, Gaby opened the book.

Wisps of smoke slowly began to curl up from the pages of the diary. Everyone, except Gaby and Catherine, took a step back. Suddenly a flash of light leaped from the page. The light began to spin faster and faster, until it became a glowing ball, darting all around the room.

"It's Ghostwriter!" Gaby cried. "He's back!"

The team and Catherine watched wide-eyed as a fully revived Ghostwriter dashed around the room, picking up letters from cardboard cartons and books until he had enough to spell out:

> You're the greatest team of all
> time!!!

"Ghostwriter!" Catherine sighed with awe. Her eyes began to fill with tears. She turned away from the team, not wanting them to see her cry. As she looked at the window above the staircase, she could have sworn she saw the strangest sight. Peering into the window were Frank and Catherine as they were in 1928. They were smiling as though they were happy to see the whole Ghostwriter Team together again.

"Are you okay?" Gaby asked as she walked over to Catherine. Catherine wiped her eyes as she turned away from the window and smiled at Gaby.

"Of course I'm okay," she said. "I'm a tough old girl."

Gaby picked the diary up from the shelf and gave it to Catherine. "You should have this," Gaby said.

"Thank you, thank you!" Catherine said softly as she and Gaby hugged.

"Hey, Catherine, come over here," Lenni called. "We want to show you our Ghostwriter cheer."

Catherine and Gaby hurried over to the rest of the team. They all got in a circle, put their hands on top of each other, and then lifted them up, cheering long and loud: "Ghoooooooostwriter!"

The swirling ball of light danced in and out and all around the team. Ghostwriter was happy to be back home.

Look for the next exciting Ghostwriter book . . .

The Ghostwriter Detective Guide 2: More Tools and Tricks of the Trade

Who's sending weird messages to the Ghostwriter Team? Solve the mystery with the clues in this cool book! Learn tricks that some of the all-time great detectives use, plus lots of other sneaky stuff, like how to

- make a decoder card so that you can send your friends secret messages
- spot counterfeit money
- get a lip print off a glass
- watch people secretly

You'll also discover tons of great new codes.

It's coming soon to a bookstore near you.